Three Masquerades

∽ಲಿಲ್ಬೇ∾

Novellas by Rachel Ingalls

THREE MASQUERADES

❧

NOVELLAS BY

RACHEL INGALLS

SELECTED AND INTRODUCED BY DANIEL HANDLER

PHAROS EDITIONS | AN IMPRINT OF COUNTERPOINT | BERKELEY

Text © 1985, 1987 by Rachel Ingalls

Introduction © 2017 by Daniel Handler

Library of Congress Cataloging-in-Publication Data is available.

Cover design by Kelly Winton
Interior design by Domini Dragoone

ISBN 978-1-94043-644-9

Pharos Editions
An Imprint of Counterpoint
2560 Ninth Street, Suite 318
Berkeley, CA 94710
www.pharoseditions.com

Printed in the United States of America
Distributed by Publishers Group West

10 9 8 7 6 5 4 3 2 1

Three Masquerades

ণ৽৻৶৽

Novellas by Rachel Ingalls

CONTENTS

INTRODUCTION

THE FICTION OF Rachel Ingalls has haunted me for years, but faced with the task of introducing her work I'm not sure what to say about it. Yet one wants to shine a light. *Mrs. Caliban*, her best-known book, is not very well known; the highest profile her work has received is that it has been adapted several times into films you likely have not seen. But while she does not loom large on the literary landscape, her work is indelible in the brain. It is easy to read and hard to forget. The plots are dramatic, even exaggerated, but the books themselves are quiet and short. They are largely about women in trouble. The language is plain but curious. One finds eerie coincidence and comic irony, a touch of the macabre. When called upon previously to describe her work, the word that came out of my mouth was "psychological," which seemed utterly meaningless the moment it was out loud. *Psychological.* What work isn't psychological? A better word might be "spooky," although that sounds too cheap for an author who often conjures a genuine sense of the unearthly.

Gathered here are three works of hers. She has been published irregularly, in different configurations, and this is another one. Two of these works are frightening and one less so, although I sometimes change my mind about which one that is. I haven't even been sure what to call them—novellas, maybe, or long short stories, that little phrase "long short" ringing as ridiculously as "psychological." So I decided to write to Ingalls—through an emissary, as she prefers—asking her a bunch of questions that come up when I think about her work, and wondering if she had a title in mind for this newly-cobbled trio. She didn't reply, and then she did. Her introduction is better than any I could muster up.

Dear Mr. Handler,

Please forgive the delay in answering your letter. Since the collapse of my Amstrad years ago, life has not been the same and until I acquire a laptop that prints from dictation, I'm stuck with an old machine I can't control and a printer I don't understand.

I'm delighted that Pharos will be publishing me, that you want to write an introduction and that you first came across my writing when you were very young—I always hope that someone out there would be reading me besides the forty or forty-five people I imagined would have heard of me.

Thank you very much for your kind words about my work. It does seem that there is some difficulty about finding a category for my books. For a while I was put in the Gothic slot but probably I'd say that a combination of fable, fairytale, and Romance would fit. Maybe that is Gothic.

As for feminism, I don't consider myself a feminist because it's a subject about which I feel ambiguous (as about so much else). I don't think that women have harder lives than men, only different, although I'm incensed by institutional misogyny which is obvious and political and, of course, unfair.

But—my main literary interest is narrative: stories, patterns, and the movement of thought. I do also love movies. When in *Jaws II* (3-D) a group of underwater scientists manage to kill a vicious whale and then find that another much bigger and fiercer whale is coming at them for revenge because it's the mother of the first one, I light up with the recognition that this is Grendel's mother from Beowulf. Yes, I value Pulp as well as other literary forms currently discounted by many critics. Melodrama, for instance, seems to me an interesting way of examining the social basis of certain emotions by exaggerating them. And farce is an ingenious method of depicting our deepest fears about identity and misunderstanding. Almost all of those '50s films are good and I grew up with them. My favorite is *The Incredible Shrinking Man*, although naturally *The Creature from the Black Lagoon* is also close to my heart. I think 'masquerade' might be a good word for one of my interests. Not quite the same word as fiction, but close.

My childhood literary influences were: being read to by my father, being told stories by him on our pre-Sunday-lunch walks, reading on my own, listening to the radio, and going to Saturday morning movie shows. The radio in America used to be marvelous—full of soap operas and jokes and lurid advertising claims. And the school I went to was wonderful, the teachers and the curriculum too.

My first ambition as a writer was to be a poet (isn't most writers'?) but after a sequence of 154 sonnets (and they all rhymed!), I had to admit that poets are born and that the sound, image, and idea come to them in an indivisible bundle that cannot be constructed. It really is a gift. Great poets think like Einstein. Most contemporary poets write broken-up pieces of prose sometimes very good and interesting and memorable, but Cole Porter or Country and Western lyrics are often better than that without pretending to be The Real Thing. My top favorite literary idols are playwrights: Shakespeare, Euripides, Ibsen.

I've never given much thought to my place among contemporary writers, nor about readers. I write because it's a compulsion. There are many, many other writers I hold dear, some living and some dead, but none of whom (after the experiments of adolescence) I'd try to emulate or imitate. When asked about writers who have influenced me, I used to cite a few but the real answer should be "all the ones I've read". I write long stories because it seems to be the length that fits what I have to say. And I know how incredibly lucky I was to find the best agent in London and the best publisher, to have anything written in novella length taken on at all and to have nothing of mine ever changed except misspelling or perhaps, very occasionally, a difficult bit of punctuation that I'd usually fight for. My books didn't sell. I was virtually carried. The only real money I've earned came from Hollywood.

So many people keep asking why I don't write a novel. Well, all that business with the subplots—it's in classical ballet too: the tragic noble love and the happy village wedding. It's even in the big symphonies. But you have to know how to make that larger idea work without dissipating the original notion or ruining the shape. Victor Hugo, Charles Dickens, Joseph Conrad—they succeeded. But *War and Peace*? Big, heroic, terrific read and yet what a mess. And *Anna Karenina* should be two separate books.

Writers who are good at publicity are good because they like it and it's easy to enjoy what you are good at, easy to be fairly good at what you enjoy. My sister tells me that a thriller writer in Boston (Robert Parker?) goes around to the bookshops there whenever he's published and he meets his fans, who adore him, and talks about his books and the characters in them and he signs books. He has a great time and so does everybody else there because he's good at social gatherings and being spontaneously entertaining. Writers like that are fun to meet. I'm not exactly a hermit but I'm really no good at meeting lots of strangers and I'd resent being set up as the new arrival in the zoo. (You see? Not a good attitude to start with. I wouldn't want to meet with that myself.) It's just that that whole clubby thing sort of gives me the creeps.

My life in England? I had a great-aunt living here for the first 11 years or so and her son's family and a few of my friends who came over on visits and then introduced me to people they knew. I didn't try to go to ground in any way. And there was always Shakespeare.

Sorry, I've left out travel but I hope this is enough. Thank you again.

—Rachel

Three Masquerades

ﾐﾟﾐﾟﾐﾟ

Novellas by Rachel Ingalls

I SEE A LONG JOURNEY

꘍꘍꘍꘍

I SEE
A LONG
JOURNEY

⧚⧚⧚⧚⧚

FLORA HAD MET James when she was going out with his younger brother, Edward. She'd been crazy about Edward, who even then had had a reputation for wildness where girls were concerned. She'd been eighteen, Edward nineteen. James was thirty-one.

She'd liked him straight away. He was easy in talking to her: relaxed and completely open, as if they'd known each other a long time. In fact, in a way she did know him already—not just through Edward, but from her older sister, Elizabeth, who had gone out with him for about two months a few years before. He had had many girlfriends and mistresses, naturally. He was agreeable and amusing, well-known everywhere and well-liked. He was also the most important of the heirs.

When he proposed to her, she thought her decision over carefully. She wasn't in love with him but she couldn't think of any reason why she should turn him down. He'd become such a good friend that she felt they were already related.

After the marriage, Edward changed along with everything else. The barriers came up all around her. Where once, on the outside, she had felt shut out of their exclusive family, now—on the inside—she was debarred from the rest of the world.

There had been a time at the beginning when she had fought. If it hadn't been for the money, she might have succeeded. Their quarrels, misunderstandings and jealousies were like those of other families. And she was like other girls who marry into a group of powerful personalities. She was tugged in different directions by all of them. They expected things of her. They criticized her. They tried to train and educate her. When she was pregnant for the first time, and when she had the child, they told her what she was doing wrong.

But that was the stage at which she found her own strength: she clung to the child and wouldn't let them near it. They had to make concessions. It was the first grand-child and a boy. She was sitting pretty. She could take her mother-in-law up on a point in conversation and make her back down.

Shortly after the birth a lot of pressure was taken off her anyway; Edward formed a liaison with a girl who sang in a nightclub. He was thinking of marrying her, he said. He wanted to introduce her to his parents—her name was Lula. His mother hit the roof about it. She described the girl as "an unfortunate creature: some sort of half-breed, I believe." Quarrels exploded over the breakfast table, down in the library, out in the garden. In the kitchen, of course, they were laughing.

She met Lula. Edward took them both out to lunch. Flora wasn't nervous about it: she even tried to put the other woman at her ease by saying that she too had once been an outsider to the family. But Lula wasn't going to accept anyone's sympathy. She put on a performance, talked loudly, looking around at the other people in the restaurant, pinched Edward under the table and went out of her way to throw as many dirty words as possible into every sentence. Then she stood up abruptly, declared that it had been so very, very nice but she had to run along now, tugged Edward by the hair and left.

"She isn't like that," he said.

"You don't have to tell me. I could see. She'll be all right when we get together next time."

"She really isn't like that."

"I know. I told you—I recognize the camouflage. I liked her fine."

"I think you made her feel unsure."

"And I'm the easy one. Wait till she meets the others. She'll have her work cut out for her."

"They gave you a rough time, I guess."

"It's all right. That's over now."

"It's mainly Mother."

"It's the whole deal."

"But things are okay between you and James?"

"Oh, yes," she said. "But we're in the thick of everything. If you and I had married, we could have escaped together."

"But we didn't love each other," he said matter-of-factly. It upset her to hear him say it. Someone should love her. Even her children—they needed her, but she was the one who did the loving.

"Besides," he told her, "I'm not sure that I want to escape. Even if it were possible. And I don't think it is."

"It's always possible if you don't have children."

He said, "It's the price of having quarterly checks and dividends, never having to work for it. Think of the way most people live. Working in a factory—could you stand it?"

"Maybe it wouldn't be so bad. If you were with somebody you loved."

"Love doesn't survive much poverty. Unless you're really right down at the bottom and don't have anything else."

Was it true? If she and her husband were lost and wandering in the desert, maybe he'd trade her for a horse or a camel, because he could always get another wife and have more children by the new one. It couldn't be true.

"I'm sure it would," she said.

"From the pinnacle, looking down," he told her, "you get that romantic blur. Wouldn't it be nice in a little country cottage with only the birds and the running streams? It's the Marie Antoinette complex."

And at another time he'd said, "Love is a luxury for us. If I were on a desert island with the soulmate of all time, I'd still have the feeling that I'd ducked out. I guess it's what they used to call 'duty.'"

"There are plenty of others to take over the duties," she'd told him.

"And they'd all think: *he wasn't up to it*. And they'd be right."

It took two years for the family to wean Edward away from Lula. Then they set him up with a suitable bride, an Irish heiress named Anna-Louise, whose family was half-German on the mother's side. One of Anna-Louise's greatest assets was that she was a superb horsewoman. Flora liked her. The boys' father, the old man, thought she was wonderful. His wife realized too late that Anna-Louise was a strong character, not to be bullied. Flora was let off the hook. She didn't allow her mother-in-law to take out on her or her children any of the failures and frustrations she had with Anna-Louise. She put her foot down. And eventually her mother-in-law came to her to seek an ally, to complain and to ask for advice. Flora listened and held her peace. She was learning.

James was the one who helped her. He guided her through her mistakes; he was the first person in her life to be able to teach her that mistakes are actually the best method of learning and that it's impossible to learn without at least some of them. He warned her about things she would have to know, strangers she was going to meet. She was grateful. But she also saw that he was part of the network and that all his actions, though well-meant, were aimed at making her just like the rest of them, whether she wanted to be or not.

It always came down to the question of money. The money made the difference. They were one of the richest families on the Eastern seaboard. Flora's own parents were from nice, substantial backgrounds; they'd had their houses and companies and clubs, and belonged to the right places when it had still been worth keeping up with that sort of thing.

She'd known people who knew the cousins, who gave parties at which she would be acceptable—that was how she had met Edward. Everyone knew about them. Everyone recognized their pictures in the papers. To marry into their ranks was like marrying into royalty, and a royalty that never had to worry about its revenues.

Her marriage had also changed her own relatives irrevocably. It was as though they had lost their thoughts and wishes; they had become hangers-on. They name-dropped with everyone, they could no longer talk about anything except the last time they'd seen James or Edward or—best of all—the old man.

They were all corrupted. One early summer afternoon Flora sat playing cards with James and Edward and her sister, Elizabeth, who had married a cousin of the family and thus, paradoxically, become less close.

Flora thought about the four of them, what they were doing with the time they had. All except for James were still in their twenties and they were like robots attached to a mastercomputer—they had no ideas, no lives. They were simply parts of a machine.

She wondered whether James and Elizabeth had slept together long ago, before she had become engaged to him, and thought they probably had. An exhaustion came over her: the artificial weariness enforced upon someone who has many capabilities and is consistently prevented from using any of them.

The doctors called it depression. She worked on her tennis, went swimming three times a week, and helped to organize charity fund-raising events. She made progress. Now she was an elegant young matron in magazine pictures, not the messy-haired girl who had run shrieking down the hallway from her mother-in-law's room as she held her squealing baby in one arm and then slammed and locked the door after her. She would never again stay behind a locked door, threatening to cut her throat, to go to the newspapers, to get a divorce. James had stood on the other side of the door and talked to her for five hours until she'd given in.

And now they had their own happy family together and she moved through the round of public and domestic duties as calmly and gracefully as a swan on the water. But the serenity of her face was like the visible after-effect of an illness she had survived; or like a symptom of the death that was to follow.

∽ↄↄↄↄ∽

JAMES THOUGHT THEY should take their holiday in a spot more remote than the ones they usually chose in the winter. He was fed up with being hounded by reporters and photographers. And she was nervous about the children all the time. The house had always received a large quantity of anonymous mail and more than the average number of unpleasant telephone cranks. Now they were being persecuted not just because of their wealth, but because it was the fashion. Every day you could read in the papers about "copy cat" crimes—acts of violence committed in imitation of something the perpetrators had seen on television or in the headlines of the very publication you had in your hand. If there had been a hoax call about a bomb at some large public building, it was fairly certain that the family secretaries would be kept busy with their share of telephone threats in the next few days. Everyone in the house was on speaking terms with at least ten policemen. There had been many crises over the years. They counted on the police, although James's mother, and his sister Margaret's ex-husband too, said they sometimes thought that most of the information these nuts and maniacs found out about them came straight from the police themselves.

Anna-Louise's entry into the family had brought further complications, adding an interest for the Irish connections on all sides. Anna-Louise herself wasn't afraid. She wasn't in any case the sort of woman who worried, but on top of that, her children hadn't been put in danger yet, whereas Margaret's had: her daughter, Amy, was once almost spirited away by a gang of kidnappers. "Fortunately," Margaret told friends later, "they got the cook's niece instead. She was standing out at the side of the back drive, and it just shows how dumb these people are: it was Sunday and she was wearing a little hat, white gloves, a pink organdy dress and Mary Janes. If they'd known anything about Amy, they'd have realized she wouldn't be caught dead in a getup like that. As a matter of fact, at that time of day on a Sunday, she'd be in her jeans, helping MacDonald in the greenhouses."

They had paid handsomely to get the niece back; good cooks weren't easy to find. But they'd cooperated with the police, which they wouldn't have dared to do if Amy herself had been the victim: it would have been too big a risk, even though in that particular case it had worked and they had caught the three men and rescued the girl. Flora later began to think it would have been better for the niece not to have lived through the capture; she started to crack up afterward and developed a bitter enmity toward Amy, who, she told everybody, ought to have been the one to be seized.

The incident had taken place when Flora was in the beginning months of her second pregnancy. It brought home to her how difficult it was to escape the family destiny: even the children were dragged into it. And though it was only one of the many frightening, uncomfortable or calamitous events from the background of her first few years of marriage, it was the one that turned her into a woman who fretted about the future and who, especially, feared for the safety of her children. James tried to soothe her. On the other hand, his friend and chauffeur, Michael, who kept telling her everything would be all right, seemed at the same time to approve of the fact that she worried. She thought he felt it was a proof that she was a good mother.

"If we go too far away," she said to James, "the children—"

"We'll have telephones and telegraphs, and an airport nearby. It isn't any worse than if we were going to California for the weekend."

"But it's so far away."

He asked, "What could we do, even here, if anything happened?" The question was meant to mollify, but it scared her even more.

"The doctor says you need a rest," he insisted. She agreed with that. It seemed odd that a woman should live in a house as large as a castle, with nothing to do all day but easy, pleasant tasks, and still need a rest. But it was true.

"Michael will be with us," he added.

That, finally, convinced her. If Michael came along, nothing bad could happen, either at home or abroad. She was distrustful of even the smallest disruption to her life, but she wanted to go. And she would be relieved to get away from the menace of all the unknown thousands who hated her without even having met her.

You couldn't be free, ever. And if you were rich, you were actually less often free than other people. You were recognized. The spotlight was on you. Strangers sent you accusations, threats and obscene letters. And what had you done to them? Nothing. Even the nice people were falsified by the ideas they had of your life; those who didn't threaten, begged. Everyone wanted money and most of them felt no shame at demanding it outright. They were sure they deserved it, so they had to have it. It didn't matter who gave it to them.

She too had been altered, of course. She had made her compromises and settled down. Of all the people connected with the family only Michael, she felt, had kept his innocence. His loyalty was like the trust of a child. When he drove her into town to shop, when they said hello or goodbye, she thought how wonderful it would be to put her arms around him, to have him put his arms around her. She was touched and delighted by all his qualities, even at the times when she'd seen him thwarted or frustrated and noticed how he went white and red very quickly.

"All right," she said. "If Michael comes too."

"Of course," James told her. "I wouldn't be without him. There's a good hotel we can stay at. I don't think you'll need a maid."

"I don't want a maid. I just want to be able to phone home twice a day to check if everything's all right."

"Everything's going to be fine. You know, sometimes kids can get sick of their parents. It won't do them any harm to miss us for a week or two."

"Two?"

"Well, if we don't make it at least two, half the trip's going to be spent in the plane, or recovering from jet-lag."

❧

THEY HAD PARTIES to say goodbye: the friends' party, the relatives', and one birthday party for Margaret's youngest child, which coincided with a garden club meeting. Flora's mother-in-law directed the gloved and hatted ladies around flowerbeds that were to be mentioned in the yearly catalogue. Her father-in-law put in a brief appearance at the far end of the Italian gardens, shook hands with a few of the women and came back to the house, where he stayed for quite a while looking with delectation at the children digging into their ice cream and cake. Flora smiled at him across the table. She got along well with him, as did all his daughters-in-law, though Anna-Louise was his favorite. His own daughters had less of his benevolence, especially Margaret, whose whole life had been, and was still, lived in the always unsuccessful effort to gain from him the admiration he gave so freely to others. That was one of the family tragedies that Flora could see clearly. No one ever said anything about it and she'd assumed from the beginning that, having grown up with it, they'd never noticed. It was simply one more truth that had become acceptable by being ritualized.

The birthday room was filled with shouts and shrieks. Food was smeared, thrown and used to make decorations. One boy had built a palace of cakes and candies on his plate. There were children of industrialists, oil millionaires, ambassadors, bankers and heads of state; but they looked just like any other children, grabbing each other's paper hats while one of them was sick on the rug.

Michael too was looking on. He was enjoying himself, but he was there to work. He watched with a professional, noting glance. If anything went wrong, he was there to stop it. His presence made Flora feel safe and happy. She began to look forward to the trip.

The next evening, it was the grownups' turn to be sick on the rug. Five of their guests had to stay over for the weekend. On Monday morning Flora and James left for the airport.

At first she'd wanted to take hundreds of photographs with her. She'd started looking through the albums and every few pages taking one or two out; then it was every other page. Finally she had a fistful of pictures, a pile as thick as a doorstop. James chose twelve, shoved the others into a drawer and told her they had to hurry now.

The children waved and smiled, their nurse cried. "I wish she wouldn't do that," Flora said in the car. "Bursting into tears all the time."

"Just a nervous habit," he told her. "It doesn't seem to affect the kids. They're a pretty hard-bitten bunch." He clasped his hand over hers, over the new ring he had given her the night before. She tried to put everything out of her mind, not to feel apprehensive about the plane flight.

They were at the airport with plenty of time to spare, so he took her arm and led her to the duty-free perfume, which didn't interest her.

"There's a bookstore," she said.

"All right."

They browsed through thrillers, war stories, romantic novels and books that claimed to tell people how society was being run and what the statistics about it proved.

They became separated. The first James knew of it was when he heard her laugh coming from the other side of the shop and saw her turn, looking for him. She was holding a large magazine.

"Come look," she called. The magazine appeared to be some kind of coloring book for children. There was a whole shelf full of the things. After the paper people in the drawings were colored and cut free, you snipped out the pictures of their clothes and pushed the tabs down over the shoulders of the dolls.

"Aren't they wonderful?" she said. "Look. This one's called 'Great Women Paper Dolls.' It's got all kinds of . . . Jane Austen, Lady Murasaki, Pavlova. Look at the one of Beatrix Potter: she's got a puppy in her arms when she's in her fancy dress, but underneath it's a rabbit. And—"

"These are pretty good," he said. He'd discovered the ones for boys: history, warfare, exploration. "As a matter of fact, the text to these things is of a very high standard. Too high for a coloring book."

"Paper doll books."

"You've got to color them before you cut them out. But anybody who could understand the information would be too old to want one. You wonder who they're aimed at."

"At precocious children like ours, of course. They'll think they're hysterical. We can send them these. Paper dolls of Napoleon and Socrates. Look, it says here: if I don't see my favorite great woman, I may find her in the book called 'Infamous Women Paper Dolls.' Oh James, help me look for that one."

"Flora," he said, "the children are here. We're the ones who are supposed to be going away."

"Yes, but we can send them right now, from the airport. Aren't they funny? Look. 'Infamous Women'—how gorgeous. Catherine di Medici, Semiramis. And in the other one—here: an extra dress for Madame de Pompadour; the only woman to get two dresses. Isn't that nice? She'd have appreciated that."

She was winding herself up to the point where at any moment her eyes would fill with tears. He said, "Who's that one? Looks like she got handed the castor oil instead of the free champagne."

"Eadburga."

"Never heard of her."

"It says she was at her worst around 802. Please, James. We can leave some money with the cashier."

"Anything to get you out of this place," he told her.

After they'd installed themselves in their seats and were up in the air, he said, "What was the difference between the great and the infamous?"

"The great were artists and heroic workers for mankind," she said. "The infamous were the ones in a position of power."

The speed of her reply took him by surprise. He couldn't remember if it might have been true. Florence Nightingale, he recalled, had figured among the greats; Amelia Earhart too. But there must also have been a ruler of some sort: Elizabeth I, maybe? Surely Queen Victoria had been in the book of good ones. And Eleanor of Aquitaine had been on a page fairly near that. He was still thinking about the question after Flora had already fallen asleep.

⁓⦿⦿⁓

THEY ARRIVED IN an air-conditioned airport much like any other, were driven away in limousines with smoked-glass windows and were deposited at their hotel, where they took showers and slept. The first thing they did when they woke up was to telephone home. They didn't really look at anything until the next day.

They walked out of the marble-pillared hotel entrance arm in arm and blinked into the sun. They were still turned around in time. Already Flora was thinking about an afternoon nap. They looked to the left and to the right, and then at each other. James smiled and Flora pressed his arm. The trip had been a good idea.

They strolled slowly forward past the large, glittering shops that sold luxury goods. You could have a set of matching jade carvings packed and sent, jewelry designed for you, clothes tailored and completed in hours. James said, "We can do all that later." Flora stopped in front of a window display of jade fruit. She said, "It's probably better to get it over with."

They stood talking about it: whether they'd leave the presents till later and go enjoy themselves, or whether they ought to get rid of the duties first, so as not to have them hanging over their heads for two weeks. Michael waited a few feet to the side, watching, as usual, without seeming to.

They decided to do the difficult presents first—the ones that demanded no thought but were simply a matter of knowing what to ask for and choosing the best. They handed over credit cards and traveler's checks for tea sets, bolts of silk material, dressing gowns, inlaid boxes, vases, bowls and bronze statuettes. By lunchtime they were worn out.

They went back to the hotel to eat. Light came into the high-ceilinged dining room through blinds, shutters, curtains and screens. It was as if they were being shielded from an outside fire—having all the heat blocked out, while some of the light was admitted. About twenty other tables were occupied. Michael sat on his own, though if they had had their meal anywhere in town, he'd have eaten with them.

James looked around and smiled again. "This is very pleasant," he said. He beamed at her and added, "I think the holiday is already doing its job. You're looking extremely well after all our shopping. Filled with a sense of achievement."

"Yes, I'm okay now. Earlier this morning I was feeling a lot like Eadburga."

"How's that?"

"At her worst around 8:15, or whenever it was."

He laughed. It had taken her years to say things that made him laugh and she still didn't know what sort of remark was going to appeal to him. Sometimes he'd laugh for what seemed to be no reason at all, simply because he was in the mood.

They went up to their rooms for a rest. She closed her eyes and couldn't sleep. He got up, shuffled through the magazines and newspapers he'd already read, and said he couldn't sleep, either. They spent the afternoon making love, instead.

"Dress for dinner tonight?" she asked as she arranged her clothes in the wardrobe.

"Let's go someplace simple. I've had enough of the well-tempered cuisine. Why don't we just slouch around and walk in somewhere?"

"You wouldn't rather get the ptomaine at the end of the trip rather than straight away?"

"Well, we've got lists of doctors and hospitals a mile long. We could get a shot for it."

"Will Michael be coming with us?"

"Of course," he said.

"Then I guess it's safe enough."

"In a pinch, I could probably protect you too."

"But you might get your suit creased." She made a funny face at him.

"I love vacations," he told her. "You're definitely at your best."

"I told you: I'm fine now."

"They say most of the jet-lag hangover is caused by dehydration, but the big difference I've noticed this time is the change in light."

"Well, it's nice to be away for a while. There'll be at least three new quarrels going by the time we get back, and they'll be missing us a lot."

"We might take more time off sometime. A long trip. A year or so."

"Oh, Jamie, all the sweat. I couldn't do it so soon again, setting up a whole new household and uprooting the children from all their friends."

"I didn't mean I'd be working. I meant just you and me away from everybody in a lovely spot, somewhere like Tahiti. New Caledonia, maybe "

She said again, "Would Michael come too?"

"I don't know. I hadn't thought."

She pulled a dress out by the hanger and decided that it wasn't too wrinkled to wear without having the hotel maid iron it.

"I guess he'd have to," James said.

"He wouldn't mind?"

"Kelvin? He never minds anything. He'd love to."

She'd have to think. If it had been Michael asking her to go away with him to the South Seas, she'd have gone like a shot. But the more dissatisfied she'd become with her life, the more reluctant she was to make any changes.

She said, "Well, it's something to think over. When would you want to make a decision about it?"

"Three weeks, about then."

"All right. We'll have to talk about the children. That's the main thing."

She was still worrying about the children as they started toward the steps that led to the elevators. There was an entire puzzle-set of interlocking staircases carpeted in pale green and accompanied by carved white banisters that made the whole arrangement look like flights of ornamental balconies. If you wanted to, you could continue on down by the stairs. James always preferred to ride in elevators rather than walk. Exercise, in his opinion, was what sport was for; it wasn't meant to move you from one place to another. Locomotion should be carried out with the aid of machines and servants.

"Let me just call home again quick," she suggested.

"You'll wake them all up. It's the wrong time there."

"Are you sure? I'm so mixed up myself, I can't tell."

"We'll phone when we get back from supper," he said.

They had been on other trips together long ago, when the telephoning had become a genuine obsession. Now they had a routine for it: she mentioned it, he told her when, she believed him and agreed to abide by the times he designated. The whole game was a leftover from the unhappy years when she'd had no self-confidence and felt that she kept doing everything wrong.

Michael stepped into the elevator after them. He moved behind them as they walked through the lobby.

"Look," Flora said.

The central fountain, which earlier in the day had been confined to three low jets, now sprayed chandelier-like cascades of brilliance into the three pools beneath. Tables and chairs had been set out around the display and five couples from the hotel were being served tea. As Flora and James watched, a group of children rushed for a table, climbed into the chairs and began to investigate the spoons and napkins. A uniformed nurse followed them.

James said, "Like some tea?"

"Unless Michael doesn't—"

"Sure," Michael said. "I'll sit right over there." He headed toward the sofas and armchairs near the reception desk. Wherever they were, he always knew where to find the best spots for surveillance, and probably had a good idea where everybody else might choose to be too. He'd been trained for all that. You couldn't see from his walk or from the way his clothes fitted that he carried guns and a knife, but he did. Sometimes it seemed incredible to Flora that he had been through scenes of violence; he'd been in the marines for two years while James was finishing up college. His placid, law-abiding face gave no sign of the fact. But she thought how upsetting the experience must have been to him at first. Even killing didn't come naturally—especially killing: somebody had to teach it to you. And boys weren't really cruel or bloodthirsty unless they had a background of brutality.

Michael's background, she knew, was quite ordinary. He was a child of an undergardener and one of the parlormaids at the house. Once she'd asked him how he'd managed to get through his military training and he'd told her that he'd been lucky: he'd been with a group of boys who'd become really good friends. And, as for violence, he'd added, "You got to be objective, say to yourself this is completely a professional thing. Like render unto Caesar. You know?" She had nodded and said yes, but had had no idea what he'd been talking about.

They sat close enough to the fountain to enjoy it but not so near as to be swept by the fine spray that clouded its outpourings. James had also taken care to station himself, and her, at a reasonable distance from the children, who looked like more than a match for their wardress.

Their nearest companions were a man and woman who might have been on a business trip or celebrating an early retirement. They gave the impression of being a couple who had been married for a long time. The woman looked older than the man. She had taken two extra chairs to hold her shopping bags and as soon as the tea was poured out she began to rummage through her papers and packages. She looked up and caught Flora's eye. Flora smiled. The woman said, "I couldn't resist. It's all so pretty and the prices are just peanuts. Aren't they, Desmond?"

The man's eyes flicked to the side. "We're going to need an extra plane to take it all back," he said. His head turned to the stairway and the main door, warily, as if looking for eavesdroppers.

"Not here," his wife told him.

"Only damn part of this hotel they let you smoke a pipe is in your own room. Place must be run by the anti-tobacco league."

"Do you good," his wife said. She began to talk about silks and jade and porcelain. Flora guessed before the woman started to quote numbers that they were going to be several price-brackets under anything she and James would have bought. On the other hand, like most rich people, she loved hunting down bargains.

The couple, whose name was Dixon, went on to tell their opinions of the city and of the country in general. They regretted, they said, not having made provision for trips outside town to—for example—the big flower festival that had been held the week before, or just the ordinary market mornings. They were leaving the next day. Flora saw James relax as he heard them say it: there wasn't going to be any danger of involvement. He began to take an interest in the list of places and shops they recommended. Flora was halfway through her second cup of tea and could tell that James would want to leave soon, when Mrs. Dixon said, "What I regret most of all, of course, is that we never got to see the goddess."

"Oh," Flora said. "At the festival?"

"At her temple."

"A statue?"

"No, no. That girl. You know—the one they train from childhood, like the Lama in Tibet."

"Not like that," her husband said.

"Well, I just couldn't face standing in line for all that time in the heat. But now I really wish I'd given myself more of a push."

"I haven't heard about the goddess," Flora admitted. James said that he'd read about it somewhere, he thought, but only remembered vaguely. And he hadn't realized that the custom had to do with this part of the world.

"Oh, yes," Mr. Dixon told him, and launched into the history of the goddess, who was selected every few years from among thousands of candidates. The child was usually four or five years old when chosen, had to be beautiful, to possess several distinct aesthetic features such as the shape of the eyes and ears and the overall proportion of the limbs, and could have no blemish. "Which is quite an unusual thing to be able to find," he said. "Then—"

"Then," Mrs. Dixon interrupted, "they train her in all the religious stuff and they also teach her how to move— sort of like those temple dancers, you know: there's a special way of sitting down and getting up, and holding out your fingers, and so on. And it all means something. Something religious. There are very strict rules she's got to obey about everything—what she can eat and drink, all that. Oh, and she should never bleed. If she cuts herself—I forget whether she has to quit or not."

"She just has to lie low for a few days, I think," Mr. Dixon said.

"And she can never cry—did I say that?"

"And never show fear."

"Then at puberty—"

"She's out on her can and that's the whole ball game. They go and choose another one."

"So people just drive out to her temple to look at her," Flora asked, "as if she's another tourist attraction?"

"Oh no, dear," Mrs. Dixon said. "They consult her. They take their troubles to her and she gives them the solution. It's like an oracle. And I think you donate some small amount for the upkeep of the temple. They don't mind tourists, but it isn't a show—it's a real religious event."

Mr. Dixon said, "She's very cultivated, so it seems. Speaks different languages and everything."

James asked, "What happens to her afterward?"

"Oh, that's the joke. She used to spend the rest of her life in seclusion as the ex-goddess. But this last time, the girl took up with a young fellow, and now she's married to him and—"

"—and there's the most terrific scandal," Mrs. Dixon said happily. "It's really turned things upside-down. I guess it's like a priest getting married to a movie star. They can't get over it."

"Matter of fact, I wouldn't want to be in that girl's shoes."

"Why?" Flora asked.

Mr. Dixon shrugged. "A lot of people are mad as hell. They've been led to expect one thing and now this other thing is sprung on them. They're used to thinking of their goddess as completely pure, and also truly sacred. I guess it can't look right for her to revert to being human all of a sudden, just like the rest of us. See what I mean?"

Flora nodded.

"She's broken the conventions," James said, which didn't seem to Flora nearly such a good explanation as Mr. Dixon's, but she smiled and nodded again.

∽ʊɞʊ∾

THEY TOOK A long time deciding where they wanted to eat their evening meal. In the beginning it was too much fun looking around to want to go inside; they had discovered the night life of the streets, full of people going about ordinary business that might have taken place indoors during the daytime: there were open-air barber shops, dress stalls where customers could choose their materials and be measured for clothes; shops that stocked real flowers and also stands that sold bouquets made out of feathers and silk.

"No wonder Mrs. Dixon had all those piles of packages," Flora said. "Everything looks so nice."

"Under this light," James warned. "I bet it's pretty tacky in daylight."

Michael grunted his assent.

"Don't you think it's fun?" she asked.

"Very colorful," he said. She wasn't disappointed in his answer. It gave her pleasure just to be walking beside him.

She would have liked to eat in one of the restaurants that were no more than just a few tables and chairs stuck out on the sidewalk. James vetoed the suggestion. They moved back to the beginning of richer neighborhoods and he suddenly said, "That one."

In front of them was a building that looked like a

joke: dragons and pagodas sprouting everywhere from its rooftops. The lower floor was plate glass, which reassured the three of them—that looked modern and therefore unromantic and probably, they expected, hygienic. "We can rough it for once," James said. Through the downstairs windows they could see rows of crowded booths, people sitting and eating. Most of the patrons appeared to be tourists—another good sign.

They entered and were seated all on the same side of a table. Flora had hoped to be put between the two men, but the waiter had positioned Michael at James's far side. Opposite her an old man was eating noodles from a bowl. He stared determinedly downward.

They looked at the menu. As James ordered for them, a young couple came up and were shown to the remaining places; he had a short beard and wore a necklace consisting of a single wooden bead strung on a leather thong; she had a long pigtail down her back. They were both dressed in T-shirts and bluejeans and carried gigantic orange backpacks. They made a big production of taking off the packs and resting them against the outside of the booth. When the old man on the inside had finished eating and wanted to get out, they had to go through the whole routine again.

Once they were settled, they stared across the table contemptuously at the fine clothes the others were wearing. They seemed to be especially incredulous over James's outfit, one which he himself would have considered a fairly ordinary linen casual suit for the tropics.

James switched from English to French and began to tell Flora about New Caledonia. It meant that Michael was excluded from the conversation, but he knew that this was one of James's favorite methods of detaching himself from company he didn't want to be associated with. It only worked in French because Flora's limited mastery of other languages wouldn't permit anything else. James had always been good at learning new languages. As a child he had even made up a language that he and Michael could use to baffle grown-up listeners. Occasionally they spoke it even now. Flora had figured out that it must be some variation of arpy-darpy talk, but it always went so fast that she could never catch anything.

The backpackers spoke English. He was American, she Australian. Their names were Joe and Irma. They spent their whole time at the table discussing the relative merits of two similar articles they had seen in different shops. Some part of the objects had been made out of snakeskin and, according to Irma, one of them was "pretty ratty-looking"; on the other one, so Joe claimed, the so-called snake had been an obvious fake, definitely plastic.

"It's like those beads you got," he said. "Supposed to be ivory, and you can see the join where they poured it into the mold in two halves and then stuck them together. Why can't you tell? How can you miss seeing it? If you keep on spending money like this—"

Irma muttered, "Well, it's my money."

"We should be keeping some by for emergencies," he said. She sulked for the rest of the meal. She chewed her food slowly and methodically. Flora wished the girl had picked everything up, thrown it all over her companion and told him to go to hell. He was staring around with disapproving interest at the other diners. He wasn't going to feel guilty about hurting his girlfriend; he hadn't even noticed her play for sympathy.

Flora said in French, "Could you really go for a year without work?"

"Sure. I'd work on something else," James said. "We'd get a nice boat, sail around." He added, "The food isn't too bad here."

"Wait till tomorrow to say it," she told him.

❧

THE WEATHER NEXT morning looked like being the start of another wonderful day. All the days were wonderful in that climate at the right time of year. They both felt fine. Michael too said he was okay. Flora called home.

She got Margaret on the line, who said, "We've missed you. Anna-Louise is on the warpath again."

"What about?"

Anna-Louise's voice came in on an extension, saying, "That isn't Margaret getting her story in first, is it? Flora?"

"Hi," Flora said. "How are you all?"

"The natives are restless, as usual."

Margaret tried to chip in but was told by Anna-Louise to get off the line. There was a click.

"Children all right?" Flora asked.

"Couldn't be better."

"Are they there?" She waved James over. They spent nearly fifteen minutes talking to the children, who said again how much they loved the paper doll books and how all their friends thought they were great and wanted some too. James began to look bored and to make motions that the conversation should stop. He leaned over Flora. "We've got to hang up now," he said into the mouthpiece.

They were the second couple into the breakfast room. "Are we that early?" she asked.

He checked his watch. "Only a little. It's surprising how many people use their holidays for sleeping."

"I guess a lot of them have jet-lag too. That's the trouble with beautiful places—they're all so far away."

He spread out the maps as Michael was seated alone at a table for two several yards beyond them. Flora had them both in view, Michael and James. She felt her face beginning to smile. At that moment she couldn't imagine herself returning from the trip. The children and relatives could stay at the other end of the telephone.

James twitched the map into place. He liked planning things out and was good at it. She, on the other hand, couldn't even fold a map back up the right way. She was better at the shopping. Now that they were used to their routines, they had a better time sightseeing. In the early days James had spent even more time phoning his broker than Flora had in worrying about the babies.

She remembered the young couple at dinner the night before, and how much they had seemed to dislike each other. Of course, it was hard to tell anything about people who were quarreling; still, they didn't seem to have acquired any of the manners and formulae and pleasing deceptions that helped to keep lovers friendly over long periods. She herself had come to believe that— if it weren't for this other glimpse of a love that would be forever unfulfilled—she'd have been content with just those diplomatic gestures, plus a shared affection for what had become familiar. If she had been free to choose at this age, her life would have been different. Everybody was free now; and they all lived together before they got married.

James put a pencil mark on the map and started to draw a line across two streets.

Maybe, she thought, she'd been free even then. The freedom, or lack of it, was simply ceremonial. Rules and customs kept you from disorder and insecurity, but they also regulated your life to an extent that was sometimes intolerable. They protected and trapped at the same time. If it weren't for habit and codes of behavior, she and Michael could have married and had a happy life together.

It had taken her years to find out that most of her troubles had been caused by trying to switch from one set of conventions to another. The people around her—even the ones who had at first seemed to be against her—had actually been all right.

She said, "You know what I'd really like to do? I'd like to see that girl."

"Hm?"

"The one the Dixons were talking about at tea. The goddess."

"Oh." James looked up. "Well, maybe. But don't you think the idea is going to be a lot better than the reality? Following it up is just going to mean what they said: standing in line for hours. Do you want to spend your vacation doing that?"

"And if you don't, regretting that you never did. I would like to. Really. You don't have to come, if you don't want to."

"Of course I'd come, if you went."

"Could you find out about it? It's the thing I want to do most."

"Why?"

"Why? Are there goddesses at home?"

He laughed, and said, "Only in the museums. And in the bedroom, if you believe the nightgown ads."

"Please."

"Okay," he promised. "I'll find out about it. But it seems to me, the one worth looking at is going to be the one that went AWOL and got married."

"She didn't go AWOL. She was retired."

"A retired goddess? No such thing. Once a god, always a god."

"If you become impure as soon as you bleed, then you can lose the divinity. Women—"

"All right, I'll find out about it today. Right now. This very minute."

"I'm only trying to explain it."

"Wasted on me," he told her.

"Don't you think it's interesting?"

"Mm."

"What does that mean?"

"I'll see about it this afternoon."

Over the next few days they went to the botanical gardens; to the theater, where they saw a long, beautiful and rather dull puppet play; and to a nightclub, at which Flora developed a headache from the smoke and James said he was pretty sure the star *chanteuse* was a man. They got dressed up in their evening clothes to visit the best restaurant in town, attended a dinner given by a friend of the family who used to be with the City Bank in the old days, and made an excursion to the boat market. Half the shops there were hardly more than floating bamboo frameworks with carpets stretched across them. Bright pink orchid-like flowers decorated all the archways and thresholds, on land and on the water. The flowers looked voluptuous but unreal, and were scentless; they added to the theatrical effect—the whole market was like a view backstage. James and Flora loved it. Michael said it was too crowded and the entire place was a fire-trap.

"Well, there's a lot of water near at hand," James said.

"You'd never make it. One push and the whole mob's going to be everybody on top of theirselves. They'd all drown together."

"I do love it when you get on to the subject of safety, Kelvin. It always makes me feel so privileged to be alive."

A privilege granted to many, Flora thought, as she gazed into the throng of shoving, babbling strangers. She suddenly felt that she had to sit down.

She turned to James. "I feel—" she began.

He saw straight away what was wrong. He put his arm around her and started to push through the crowd. Michael took the other side. She knew that if she really collapsed, Michael could pick her up and sling her over his shoulder like a sack of flour, he was so strong. He'd had to do it once when she'd fainted at a ladies' fund-raising luncheon. That had been a hot day too, lunch with wine under a blue canvas awning outdoors; but she'd been pregnant then. There was no reason now for her to faint, except the crowd and the lack of oxygen.

There wasn't any place to sit down. She tried to slump against Michael. They moved her forward.

"Here," James said.

She sat on something that turned out to be a tea chest. They were in another part of the main arcade, in a section that sold all kinds of boxes and trunks. A man came up to James, wanting to know if he was going to buy the chest.

Back at the hotel, they laughed about it. James had had to shell out for a sandalwood casket in order to give her time to recover. When they were alone, he asked if she was really all right, or could it be that they'd been overdoing it in the afternoons? She told him not to be silly: she was fine.

"I think maybe we should cancel the trip to the goddess, though, don't you?"

"No, James. I'm completely okay."

"Waiting out in the sun—"

"We'll see about that when we get there," she said flatly. It was a tone she very seldom used.

"Okay, it's your vacation. I guess we could always carry you in on a stretcher and say you were a pilgrim."

He arranged everything for the trip to the temple. The day he chose was near the end of their stay, but not so close to the flight that they couldn't make another date if something went wrong. One of them might come down with a twenty-four-hour bug or there might be a freak rainstorm that would flood the roads. "Or," James said, "if she scratches herself with a pin, we've had it till she heals up. They might even have to choose a new girl."

In the meantime they went to look at something called "the jade pavilion"—a room in an abandoned palace, where the silk walls had been screened by a lattice-work fence of carved jade flowers. The stone had been sheared and sliced and ground to such a fineness that in some places it appeared as thin as paper. The colors were vibrant and glowing—not with the freshness of real flowers nor the sparkle of faceted jewels, but with the luster of fruits; the shine that came off the surfaces was almost wet-looking.

As they walked under the central trellis a woman behind them said, "Think of having to dust this place." A man's voice answered her, saying, "Plenty of slave labor here. Nobody worries about dust."

"Glorious," James said afterward. And Michael declared that, "You had to hand it to them." He'd been impressed by the amount of planning that must have gone into the work: the measuring and matching, the exactitude.

Flora had liked the silk walls behind, which were covered with pictures of flying birds. She said, "I guess you're supposed to think to yourself that you're in a garden, looking out. But it's a little too ornate for me. It's like those rooms we saw in Palermo, where the whole place was gold and enamel—like being inside a jewel box. This one would have been even nicer made out of wood and then painted. Don't you think?"

"That would fade," James said. "You'd have to re-do it all the time. And in this climate you'd probably need to replace sections of it every few years."

They kept calling home every day. The weather there was horrible, everyone said. Anna-Louise had a long story about friends of hers whose house had been burgled. And one of the children had a sore throat; he coughed dramatically into the receiver to show how bad it was.

"They need us," Flora said. "That was a cry of despair."

"That was the standard performance," James told her. "There's one who hasn't inherited any bashfulness. He'd cough his heart out in front of fifty reporters every day and do retakes if he thought it hadn't been a really thorough job. No hired substitute for him. It's going to be a question of how hard we'll have to sit on him to keep him down. Worse than Teddy was at that age."

"He sounded pretty bad."

"You're the one we're going to worry about at the moment. One at a time. Feeling faint? Claustrophobic?"

Flora shook her head. She felt fine. They strolled around town together and sat in a public park for a while. They'd chosen a bench within the shade of a widely branched, symmetrical tree. Michael rested against the stonework of a gate some distance away. While he kept them in sight, he watched the people who passed by. James pointed out a pair of tourists coming through the entrance.

"Where?" Flora asked.

"Right by the gate. It's those two from the restaurant we went to our first night out."

"Irma and Joe," she said. "So it is. And they're still arguing. Look."

The couple had come to a stop inside the gates. Joe leaned forward and made sweeping gestures with his arms. Irma held herself in a crouching posture of defense: knees bent, shoulders hunched, chin forward. Her fists were balled up against her collarbone. The two faced each other still encumbered by their backpacks and bearing a comical resemblance to armored warriors or wrestlers costumed in heavy padding.

James said, "She's just spent all her money and he's bawling her out."

"You give it to him, Irma," Flora said. James squeezed her hand.

They stayed on their bench and watched a large group of uniformed schoolchildren who—under the supervision of their teachers—went through what seemed to be the usual class exercises and then began to play some game neither Flora nor James could understand. Two of the children passed a book through the group while the others counted, telling off certain players to skip in a circle around the rest. Then they all sang a rhyming verse and formed up in a new order.

At last he said, "Okay?" and stood up. She got to her feet. In the distance Michael too stepped forward.

They were three streets from where the hired car was parked, when Flora caught sight of a yellow bowl in a store window. She slowed down and, briefly, paused to look. James and Michael moved on a few paces. She turned back, to ask James what he thought about the bowl, and a hand closed gently over her arm just above the wrist. She looked up into a face she'd never seen before. For a moment she didn't realize anything. Then the hand tightened. At the same time, someone else grabbed her from behind. She dropped her handbag. Gasping and mewing sounds came from her throat, but she couldn't make any louder noise. She tried to kick, but that was all she could do.

Michael and James were with her almost immediately, hitting and kicking. Michael actually threw one of the gang into the air. Flora felt herself released. She fell to her knees, with her head against the glass of the window.

"Here," James said, "hold on to that." He thrust her handbag into her arms and pulled her back up. She still couldn't speak.

They hurried her to the car and drove back to the hotel. Michael came up to the room with them and sat on the edge of the bed. James said he was calling in a doctor.

"I'm all right," she jabbered, "all right, perfectly—I'm fine. I'm just so mad. I'm so mad I could chew bricks. The nerve of those people!" She was shaking.

Michael stood up and got her a glass of water. She drank all of it and put her head down on the bed.

"That's a good idea," James said. He and Michael left her and went into the sitting room. She could hear them talking. Michael said, "The cops?" and James said, "Tied up with police on vacation. Besides, what good?"

"No hope," Michael answered. "Anyway, weren't after money."

"Bag."

"No, arm. And left it. Her, not the. Alley right next. A few more seconds."

"Jesus Christ," James said. "That means."

Michael's voice said, "Maybe not," and Flora began to relax. She slept for a few minutes. She was on a beach in New Caledonia and Michael was sitting beside her on the sand. There was a barrel-vaulted roof of palm leaves overhead, like the canopy of a four-poster bed. She could hear the sound of the sea. And then suddenly someone stepped up in back of her and her arms were grabbed from behind.

She woke up. She almost felt the touch still, although

it had been in her dream. She stared ahead at the chairs by the bed, the green-and-yellow pattern of the material they were upholstered in, the white net curtains over the windows where the light was beginning to dim away. She thought about the real event, earlier in the afternoon, and remembered again—as if it had left a mark on her body— the moment when the hand had closed over her arm. Once more she was filled with outrage and fury. *The nerve,* she thought; *the nerve.* And the terrible feeling of having been made powerless, of being held, pinioned, captured by people who had no right to touch her. That laying of the hand on her had been like the striking of a predator, and just as impersonal. When she thought about it, it seemed to her that she was picturing all the men as much bigger and stronger than they probably were, and perhaps older too. They might have been only teenagers.

She wanted to forget about it. It was over. And James was right: it would ruin what was left of their trip to spend it making out reports in a police station. What could the police do? These gangs of muggers hit you, disappeared around a corner and that was the end of the trail. Once in Tokyo she and James had seen a man on the opposite side- walk robbed by two boys. His hands had suddenly gone up in the air; and there was the pistol right in broad daylight, pointing into his chest. It could happen so fast. It was the kind of street crime she had come on the holiday in order to forget.

But you had to be prepared. These things were international. And timeless. All the cruelties came back: torture, piracy, massacres. The good things didn't return so often because it took too long to develop them. And it took a whole system of convention and ritual to keep them working; wheels within wheels. She was part of it. To keep the ordered world safe, you had to budget for natural deterioration, and the cost of replacement. Nothing had a very high survival rate—not even jade, hard as it was.

She thought about the pavilion of jade flowers and wondered whether it was really so beautiful. Maybe in any case it was only as good as the people who liked it believed it to be. James had loved it. Michael hadn't seemed to like it except for the evidence of the work that had been put into it. He might have disapproved of the extravagance rather than been judging the place on aesthetic grounds. She felt herself falling asleep again.

When she woke it was growing dark. She got up, took a shower and changed. The three of them ate together in the hotel dining room, drank a great deal, had coffee and then even more to drink afterward. They talked about law and order and decent values and Flora was tight enough to say, "We can afford to." They agreed not to mention the incident to anyone at home until the trip was over.

James had a hangover the next day but read through all his newspapers as usual.

"Any mention of our little drama?" she asked.

"Of course not. We didn't report it. A few other muggings here, it says."

"Maybe they're the same ones."

"Nope. They'd have gone for the bag and left you. These are all cases of grab-and-run."

"You mean, they wanted to kidnap me; get you to pay ransom. So, they must know all about us, who we are, what you can raise at short notice."

"Maybe they check up on everybody staying at big hotels. Maybe they saw your rings. Or it might just be that they know a good-looking woman when they see one: probably thought they could sell you to somebody."

"What?"

"Sure. Hey, look what else. It says here, the ex-goddess was stoned outside her house yesterday morning."

"Yesterday morning we were pretty stoned too. Or was that this morning?"

"A mob threw stones at her. They were some kind of religious group."

"That's disgusting. That's even worse than trying to kidnap people."

"She's all right, but she's in the hospital. That ought to mean she's okay. It only takes one stone to kill somebody."

"Disgusting," Flora muttered.

"And interesting," James said. "In a lot of countries it's still the traditional punishment for adultery."

❧❧❧

THEIR HIRED CAR drove them down the coastline. They took a picnic lunch, went for a swim and visited two shrines that, according to their guidebooks, were famous. On the next day they spent the morning trying to find material for curtains to go in a house belonging to Elizabeth's mother-in-law. Michael kept close to Flora all the time; their clothes often brushed as they walked or stood side by side.

On the day of their visit to the goddess it looked for the first time during the trip as if it might rain. James went back up to their rooms and got the umbrellas. On the ride out into the country they heard a few rumblings of thunder, but after that the skies began to clear and the day turned hot and muggy. The umbrellas sat in the car while they entered the temple precincts.

They were checked at the main gate, which looked more like the entrance to a fortress than to a religious building. Flora saw James stiffen as he caught sight of the long row of invalids sitting or lying on their sides, their relatives squatting near them on the ground. She remembered his joke about pilgrims. It wasn't so funny to see the real thing. He never liked being in places where there might be diseases. Most of their traveling had been carefully packaged and sanitized to avoid coming into contact with contagion or even the grosser aspects of simple poverty. You could have all the shots you liked, and it wouldn't help against the wrong virus. She knew that he'd be telling himself again about the number and quality of the hospitals in town.

The officials looked at their papers, spoke to the driver and interpreter, and let them in. The pilgrims stayed outside on the ground. Flora wondered how long they'd have to wait, and how important it was to pay over money before you were granted an interview; or maybe the goddess did a kind of group blessing from a distance. If she wasn't even allowed to bleed, she might not be any more eager than James to get close to the diseased masses. Even when inside the courtyard you could hear a couple of them from over the wall, coughing their lungs out. The smell of decay that hung around the place might have been coming from the same source.

They were escorted across a vast, open space, through an archway, into another courtyard, across that, and to a third. The long-robed official then led them up on to the porch of one of the side buildings, around the verandah and into an assembly hall. It felt dark and cool after the walk in the open. About seventy people waited inside, some sitting on the floor and others—mainly Western tourists—either on the built-in wood bench that ran around three of the walls, or on fold-up seats they'd brought with them. There were also low stools you could borrow or rent from the temple.

The official swept forward toward a door at the far end of the hall. Two more robed figures stood on guard by it. Flora's glance flickered lightly over the other people as she passed. There weren't many children there, except for very small babies that had had to be taken along so the mother could feed them. Most of the believers or curiosity-seekers were grown up and a good proportion of them quite old. A lot of them were also talking, the deaf ones talking loudly. Perhaps the fact that one figure was on its own, not turned to anyone else, was what made Flora notice: there, sitting almost in the middle of the dark wooden floor, was Irma, resting her spine against her backpack. Joe wasn't with her. And she looked defeated, bedraggled, lost. Maybe she'd come not because this was a tourist attraction, but because she needed advice. She still looked to Flora like the complete guru-chaser—one of those girls who went wandering around looking for somebody to tell them the meaning of life. Yet she also looked desperate in another way, which Flora thought might not have anything to do with religion or philosophy or breaking up with a boy-friend, and might simply be financial. She was so struck by the girl's attitude that she almost forgot about the goddess.

They were rushed onward. The sentries opened the double doors for them and they went through like an awaited procession, entering and leaving three more hall-ways, all empty and each quieter than the last, until they reached a room like a schoolroom full of benches, and were asked to sit down. Their officials stepped forward to speak with two middle-aged priestesses who had come out of the chamber beyond—perhaps the place where the goddess was actually sitting. The idea suddenly gave Flora the creeps. It was like visiting a tomb.

She whispered to James, "Did you see Irma out there?"

"Yes."

"I'm glad she's split up with him, but she looks terrible. I think she must be broke."

"Probably."

"I'd like to give her something."

"No."

"Not much, just—"

It would mean so little to them, Flora thought, and so much to the girl. It would be even better to be able to tell her she'd done the right thing in leaving that boy and could choose a different man now if she wanted to, and this time find one who'd really love her.

James said, "You've got to let people lead their own lives."

Of course, it was assuming a lot. Irma might not have broken up with Joe at all. They might be meeting again in the evening after seeing the sights separately. Even so, it was certainly true that she had run out of money. There had to be some way of helping her out, but Flora couldn't think of one. Could she just hand over some cash and say, "Did you drop this?" Maybe she could say, "We were in the restaurant that night and you must have left this behind, it was lying in the corner of the seat and we've been looking for you ever since."

"She'll fall on her feet," James told her.

"For heaven's sake. It looks like she's fallen on her head. Can't we do something?"

"I don't think so. And I don't think we should. But if you still feel the same after we get through with this, we'll see. You'll have to figure out how to work it. And don't invite her back in the car."

Flora stared upward, thinking. She saw for the first time that the ceiling beams were carved at regular intervals with formal designs and they were painted in colors so bright that they looked like enamelwork. She'd been right; that kind of thing was much more interesting than the jade pavilion. She thought: *I'll just put some bills into an envelope and use the story about finding it in the restaurant.* It was a shame when people ignored their good intentions because it was too difficult or too embarrassing to carry them out. She usually kept a few envelopes in her pocketbook.

The interpreter came back to their bench. "Who is the seeker of truth?" he asked.

Flora looked blank. James said, "What?"

"Is it you both two or three ask the goddess, or how many?"

"Just one," James said. "My wife."

The man withdrew again. He spoke to the priestesses. One of them clapped her hands, the other went into the next room. The robed official spoke.

"Arise, if you please," the interpreter told them. Michael moved from his bench to stand behind James. The three of them stepped forward until the official put up his hand against them.

The priestess came out again, leading a procession of eight women like herself. They walked two by two. In the middle of the line, after the first four and in front of the next four they'd kept a free space, in which trotted a midget-like, pink-clad figure: the goddess herself.

She was like a ceremonial doll only taken out on special occasions. Her robes reached to the floor. On her head she wore an elaborate triple-tiered crown of pearls and rubies and some sparkling grayish glass studs that were probably old diamonds. Long, wide earrings dangled from her ears and continued the framing lines of the ornamentation above, so that the still eyes seemed to float among the shimmering lights of crown, earrings, side panels and many-stranded necklaces.

All dressed up, just like a little lady, Flora thought; *what a dreadful thing to do to that child.* And yet the face that gazed out of all its glittering trappings was not exactly that of a child: enormous, dark eyes; serenely smiling mouth; the lovely bone-structure and the refinement of the features were like those of a miniature woman, not a child. Above all, the look of utter calmness and wisdom were strange to see. The girl could have been somewhere between seven and eight years old, although she was about the size of an American child of five.

The procession stopped. The official beckoned to Flora. She came up to where he pointed. The child, who hadn't looked at anything particular in the room, turned to her with pleased recognition, like a mother greeting a daughter.

Flora bowed and smiled back, slightly flustered but tingling with gratification. *This is weird,* she thought. *This is ridiculous.* But as the procession wheeled around, heading back into the room it had come from and gathering her along with it, she knew she would follow wherever they went and for however long they wanted her to keep going. She was actually close to tears.

The room was not a room, only another corridor. They had to walk down several turnings until they emerged at a courtyard of fruit trees. They entered the audience chamber from the far side.

The goddess seated herself on a wooden throne raised on steps. Like the rafters in this room too, the throne was carved and painted. She sat on a cushion of some ordinary material like burlap, which made her robes appear even more luxurious by contrast. Her tiny feet in their embroidered magenta slippers rested on one of the steps.

A robed woman, who had been waiting for them in the room, came and stood behind and a little to the side of the throne like a governess or a chaperone. Flora wondered if in fact the woman was to be the one to hand out the answers.

The little girl smiled prettily and said, "Please sit." She indicated the hassock in front of the steps to the throne. Flora knelt. She was uncomfortable. Her skirt felt too tight and her heart was thumping heavily. She raised her glance to the child and met, from out of all the silks and jewels, a look of happy repose.

"Speak freely," the child told her in a musical voice. "And say what is in your heart."

Flora swallowed. She could hear the loud sound it made in her throat. All at once tears were in her eyes. She saw the figure before her in a blur, as if it might have been a holy statue and not a human being.

She began, "I don't know what to do. Year after year. My life is useless. I have everything, nothing to want. Kind husband, wonderful children. I feel ashamed to be ungrateful, but it never was what . . . it never seemed like mine. It's as if I'd never had my own self. But there's one thing: a man. He's the only one who isn't corrupted, the only one I can rely on. I think about him all the time. I can't stop. I can't stand the idea that we'll never be together. He's only a servant. And I don't know what to do. I love him so much." She ended on a sob and was silent.

She waited. Nothing happened. She sniffed, wiped the back of her hand across her cheek and looked up for her answer.

"Love?" the goddess asked.

Flora nodded. "Yes," she mumbled. "Yes, yes."

"True love," the sweet voice told her, "is poor."

Poor? Flora was bewildered. *Pure,* she thought. *Of course.*

"It is from the sky."

The chaperone leaned forward toward the jeweled head. "Godly," she hissed.

"Godly?" the child repeated, smiling into Flora's anxious face. The densely embellished right sleeve raised itself as the girl lifted her arm. The small hand made a lyrical gesture up toward the heavens and back in an arc to the ground: a movement that described beauty and love falling upon human lovers below, uniting as it touched them—bringing together, inevitably, her life and Michael's without greed or insistence.

"Yes, yes," she stammered again. She felt stunned. She knew that she had had her answer, whatever it was. It would take her some time to figure out exactly what it meant.

The child hadn't finished. "You must rise above," she said thoughtfully. "You must ascend."

"Transcend," the chaperone corrected.

"Ascend," the child repeated.

Flora nodded. She sighed and said, "Thank you." She started to get up. The chaperone came forward and, without touching, showed her the directions in which she should go. For a moment the woman blocked any further sight of the child. She indicated that Flora should move away, not try to catch another glimpse of the goddess, not to say thank you again; the interview was over.

She walked clumsily from the chamber and staggered a few times as she followed two priestesses back to the waiting-room. She bowed farewell to everyone. She let James take her by the arm. As they were ushered out, she leaned against him.

As soon as they passed outside the main gates, he began to hurry her along.

"Why are we going so fast?" she complained.

"Because you look terrible. I want to get you back into the car. You look like you're ready to faint again."

"You're going too fast. I can't keep up."

"Try, Flora," he said. "We can carry you if we have to."

"No."

"Christ knows why I let you talk me into this. What did she do—say she saw the ace of spades in your palm, or something? Jesus." He and Michael bundled her into the car and they started on the drive to town.

She fell back in the seat. She still couldn't think clearly. *I must ascend,* she thought. It might be painful, but it would be necessary. *Did she mean that I have to rise above earthly love?* Maybe what the goddess had meant was that in the end everyone died and went to heaven, so it wasn't worth getting upset over unimportant things.

And perhaps the girl had also meant exactly what she'd said about love—that it was from heaven, freely given and necessary, but that rich people never had to feel necessity; if a friendship broke down, or a marriage, or a blood relationship, they somehow always managed to buy another one. Life could be made very agreeable that way. But love was what the goddess had said it was—not pure: poor.

"Well?" James asked.

"Better," she said.

"Thank God for that. What did the creature do to you?"

"She told me I had to rise above."

"Rise above what?"

"Oh, everything, I guess."

"And that's what knocked you out—the Eastern version of moral uplift?"

"I just suddenly felt sort of . . . I don't know."

He bent toward her, kissed her near her ear and whispered, "Pregnant."

"No."

"Sure? You've been close to fainting twice."

"Yes," she said. "Yes, I'm sure. No. What did you think of it all, Michael?"

"Very interesting indeed," Michael answered. "It's another way of life."

"What did you think of her? The goddess."

"Cute-looking little kid, but skinny as a rail underneath all those party clothes. You wonder if they feed them enough."

"Those hundreds of people on litters believe she can cure them."

"Yeah, well, they're sick. Sick people believe in anything."

"Maybe they're right. Sometimes if you have faith, it makes things true."

James groaned slightly with impatience.

Michael said, "It's deception. Self-deception always makes people feel good. But it wouldn't fix a broken leg, if that's what was wrong with you. It might help you get better quicker, once a doctor's done the real work—see what I mean?"

"Yes, I see," she said. He didn't understand. But there was no reason why he should. James said that she was tired and upset. "We'll be back soon," he assured her. "And let's have an early lunch. I'm hungry as hell from getting up so early."

"Is it still morning? You didn't think much of her, either, did you?"

"I thought she looked great, really fabulous—the dress, like a walking cyclamen plant, and the whole effect very pretty but a bit bizarre: like a gnome out of a fairy tale. What I don't like is how she's knocked the wind out of you. They aren't supposed to do that. They're supposed to give comfort and strength. That's the nature of the job."

"She did. She gave me something to think about, anyway. All the rest was me trying to get out what I wanted to say."

He held her hand. He didn't ask what her request had been. He probably thought he knew; he'd think she'd have wanted to know something like, "Why can't I be happy?" Everybody wanted happiness.

The car speeded up along the stretches by the coastline. They opened the windows and got a whiff of the sea before returning to the air-conditioning. Flora breathed deeply. All beaches were the same: salt and iodine, like the summers of her childhood. New Caledonia would be like this too.

They reached town before noon. James ordered the car to wait down a side street. The three of them got out and walked to one of the nice restaurants they had tried several times before. Flora was all right now, except that she felt bemused. She could walk without any trouble but she couldn't stop thinking about the temple and the goddess. She especially couldn't stop remembering the expression of joyful serenity on the child's face. It seemed to her that if she kept up the attempt to recapture the way it looked, she wouldn't have to let go of it.

The whole business had gone very quickly, as matters usually did when well-organized, and paid for, in advance. And now they were having a good meal in a comfortable restaurant; and only at that moment did Flora recall that she'd meant to go up to Irma on her way out and hand her some money in an envelope.

"Eat," James said.

She shook her head.

"Just a little," he insisted.

She picked up the china spoon and looked at it. She put it into the soup bowl. James watched patiently. When the children had been small, he was always the one who could make them eat when they didn't want to, and later, make them brush their teeth: he let you know, without saying anything, that he was prepared to wait forever, unchanging and with arms folded, until you did the right thing. Authority. And he never bothered with modern ideas about explaining things rationally. If the children asked, "Why do I have to?" he'd answer, "Because I say so."

She began slowly, then ate hungrily. Before the coffee, she went off to the ladies' room for a long time and while she was there made sure that her face and hair looked perfect. She even thought of brushing her teeth with the traveling toothbrush she carried in her purse, but she'd be back at the hotel soon—she could do it there. James smiled approvingly as she emerged.

They sauntered out into the hot, dusty street again.

"Museum?" he suggested, "or siesta?"

"A little nap might be nice. Is that all right with you, Michael?"

"Sure, fine," Michael said.

James stopped on the corner. "Where was that museum, anyhow?" he asked. "Down around that street there somewhere, isn't it?"

Michael looked up. He began to point things out in the distance. Flora kept walking around the bend as the street curved to the right. She drew back against the buildings to avoid three boys who were standing together and talking in whispers. But as soon as she was clear, two others came out of a doorway. She started to move away, but they came straight toward her. And suddenly the first three, their friends, were behind her, snatching at her arms. It was the same as the day before, but this time she screamed loudly for Michael before the hands started to grip over her eyes and mouth. She also kicked and thrashed while they dragged her along the sidewalk. Right at the beginning, except for her own outburst, all the violent pulling and shoving took place to the accompaniment of low mutters and hisses. Only when James and Michael came charging around the corner did the real noise begin.

The gang had guns. The man now left alone to hold Flora from behind was jabbing something into her backbone. She knew it was a gun because she saw two of the others pull out pistols. They went for James. The voice behind her yelled, "Stop, or we kill the woman." Flora kept still, in case her struggling caused the weapon to go off by mistake. But Michael had his own gun in his hand and was crouched down in the road. He shot the two who were heading toward James, the third, who was waving a pistol in the air, and there was a fourth explosion landing some-place where Flora couldn't see. The arm around her gripped so tightly that she was suffocating. The voice, sounding deranged, screamed into her ear, "You drop the gun, or I kill her!" She knew he meant it. He'd do anything. He might even kill her without knowing what he was doing.

Michael didn't hesitate. She saw him turn toward them and the look on his face was nothing: it was like being confronted by a machine. He fired right at her. She should have known.

She didn't fall straight away. The man who had held her lay dead on the ground while she swayed above him. She knew she'd been shot, but not where. It felt as if she'd been hit by a truck. And suddenly she saw that there was blood everywhere—maybe hers, maybe other people's.

She should have known that a man formed by the conventions of the world into which she had married would already have his loyalties arranged in order of importance, and that the men and male heirs to the line would always take precedence over the outsiders who had fitted themselves into their lives. James was central; she was only decoration. As long as one man in the street was left with a gun, that was a danger to James. In Michael's eyes she had passed during less than three minutes from object to obstacle. He'd shot her to pieces, and, using her as a target, killed the gunman behind her.

James had his arms around her. He was calling out for an ambulance. There were plenty of other people on the street now. And she thought: *My God, how embarrassing: I've wet my pants.* But what she said was, "I'm bleeding," and passed out.

∝ჿჿᏰᏰᏝ

SHE WOKE UP looking at a wall, at window-blinds, at the ceiling. Everything hurt.

It was still daylight, so perhaps she hadn't been there very long. Or maybe it was the next day. It felt like a long time. She was trussed like a swaddled baby and she was hooked up to a lot of tubes—she could see that too. And she was terrified that parts of her body had been shattered beyond repair: that they would be crippled so badly that they'd never move again, that perhaps the doctors had amputated limbs. The fear was even worse than the pain.

Someone got up from behind all the machinery on her other side and left the room.

James came from around the back of her bed and sat in a chair next to her. He looked tired. And sad too. That was unusual; she'd hardly ever seen him looking sad. He reached over and put his hand on her bare right arm, which lay outside the covers. She realized that she must be naked underneath; only bandages, no nightgown.

"You're going to be all right," he told her.

She believed him. She said, "Hurts a lot." He smiled grimly. She asked, "How long have I been here?"

"Twenty-four hours."

"You haven't shaved."

He kept squeezing her arm lightly and looking into her face. She thought she was about to go back to sleep again, but he caught her attention by saying her name.

"Would you do something for me?"

She said, "Of course. You're always so good to me."

He put his head down on the bed for a while and sighed. He really did love her, she thought, but she'd never believed it before.

"If you could talk to Michael," he said. "Just a couple of seconds. He feels so broken up about how it happened. If you could just let him know you understand."

"I understand," she said.

"I mean, tell him you forgive him. He hasn't said much, but he hasn't been able to eat or sleep, either. Or shave. Can I tell him to come in?"

She suddenly sensed that everything was draining away from her, never to return. She tried to hold on, but it was no use.

"Flora?"

The horror passed. She felt better. The fear had left, along with all the rest. She knew that she was going to die.

"Yes," she said. "Tell him to come in."

James went away. She heard his footsteps. And Michael's; heard James saying, "Just a couple of seconds. She's very tired," and saw him moving away out of the room as Michael sat down in the chair. She turned her head to look at him.

He was smiling. Even with her head to the side, she could see his expression exactly: a nasty little smile. His drunken uncle had been chauffeur and pander to the old man and his cousins; and, of course, Michael would have taken over the same office for the sons. She should have known. It was that kind of family: even the employees were inheritable.

Everything was obvious now, and especially the fact that Michael's unshakable politeness and deference had been an indication of his distaste for her. He'd given up pretending, now that he knew she was dying. It was more than distaste. It must be a real hatred, because he couldn't help it any longer. He wanted to show her, even with James just outside the door.

"I want you to understand," he said quietly.

"No need," she answered.

"You got to understand, it's for him. Far as I'm concerned, I don't give a shit. You've just got to tell him you forgive me. Then it'll be okay."

Everything would be all right. It was simple, if you had that much money. When they reported the attack, James would see to it that everyone thought she'd been shot by the kidnappers, not by Michael. Who would question it? Two respectable witnesses; and dead men who were known criminals. The hospital would get a new wing, the police force a large donation. It would be easy. It would have been easy even if they'd deliberately set out to murder her and hired the men to do it.

"If it was me," Michael said, leaning forward, "I'd be counting the minutes till you go down the tubes. 'Oh James dear, look at that, oh isn't that perfectly sweet? Can I have the car window open, if it's all right with Michael:

can I have it closed, if Michael doesn't mind?' Pain in the ass is what you are. I mean, I seen plenty: one to a hundred I used to mark them, and you rate down around ten, sweetheart. A real lemon. 'Am I doing this right, am I doing that?' I told him, 'Jimbo, this one's a dud.' And he just said, 'No, Kelvin, this time I'm choosing for myself.' He wouldn't listen."

James could do it right next time, she thought. He'd marry again, perhaps quite soon, and be just as content. He'd probably go to New Caledonia after all, maybe with another woman, or just with Michael. Someone else would bring up her children, no doubt doing it very well. They'd have the photographs of her, so everyone could remember how pretty she'd been; she had always taken a good picture. The family would be able to choose the new wife, as they'd chosen for Edward. She'd been crazy about Edward; that was how everything had started. It was enough to make you laugh. But she had to stop thinking about it. She had to ascend. All the events in the house and all the holiday traveling would still go on, only she wouldn't be able to have any part in them. She had to rise above.

"I forgive," she said. It was becoming difficult for her to speak.

"I'll get him," Michael told her. He stood up.

"Wait." She started to breathe quickly.

He leaned across the bed to look at her face. He said, "I'll get somebody."

"Michael," she said clearly, "I loved you."

He stepped back. The smile vanished. He looked revolted, infuriated.

"I loved you," she repeated. "With all my heart." Her lips curved together, her eyes closed, her head moved to the side. She was gone.

Michael began to scream.

The sound brought James running into the room, and two nurses after him.

Michael caught Flora up in his arms. He shouted into her closed face. He tried to slam her against the wall. James pulled him back. "It's all right," he said. "Stop."

"Bitch," Michael yelled at Flora. "Take it back. Take it back, you lousy bitch."

"Calm down," James said. "She forgives you." He got his arm around both of them and tugged. Michael let go, dropping Flora's body. She fell face downward. The nurses stooped to pick her up from the floor.

James and Michael stood grappled together, their faces wet with tears and sweat. Michael stared at the wall in front of him.

"It's all right," James told him. "She understands. Don't worry. After people die, they understand everything."

FRIENDS IN THE COUNTRY

∾ು౫౫ಀ

FRIENDS IN THE COUNTRY

꙰

IT TOOK THEM an hour to leave the house. Jim kept asking Lisa where things were and why she hadn't bought such and such; if she'd intended to buy that thing there, then she should have warned him beforehand. "Otherwise," he told her, "we duplicate everything and it's a waste of money. Look, now we've got two flashlights."

She let the shopping bag drop down on the floor with a crash. "Right. That's one for you and one for me," she said. "And then we won't have to argue about it when we split up."

His face went set in an expression she recognized. He'd skipped two intermediate phases and jumped to the stage where, instead of being hurt, he started to enjoy the battle and would go for more provocation, hoping that they'd begin to get personal. "In that case," he said, "I choose the blue one."

She laughed. She leaned against the wall, laughing, until he had to join in. He said, "We can keep the black one in the car, I guess. It might come in useful."

"You think we should phone them?"

He shook his head. He didn't know anything about this Elaine—she was Nancy's friend—but he was pretty sure her cousin wouldn't want to begin eating before eight on a Friday night, especially not if she lived out of town. "And they shouldn't anyway," he added. "Eight-thirty would be the right time."

"But some people do. If you're working nine to five, and if you—"

"Then they ought to know better."

There were further delays as he wondered whether to take a bottle of wine, and then how good it had to be if he did. Lisa heard him rooting around in the kitchen as she stared closely into the bathroom mirror. She smeared a thin film of Vaseline on the tips of her eyelashes, put her glasses on, took them off and leaned forward. Her nose touched the glass. Jim began to yell for her to hurry up. Her grandfather used to do the same thing; she could remember him shouting up the stairs for her grandmother; and then if there was still no result, he'd go out and sit in the car and honk the horn. Jim hadn't learned that extra step yet, but he might think of it at any minute. They'd been living together for only a few months. She was still a little worried that one day he might get into the car and drive off without her.

They were out of the house, in the car, and halfway down the street when she remembered that she'd left the bathroom light on. She didn't say anything about it. They moved on toward the intersection. Jim was feeling good, now that they'd started: the passable bottle of wine being shaken around in the backseat, the new flashlight in the glove compartment. He looked to the left and into the mirror.

She tried not to breathe. She always hated the moment of decision—when you had to hurl your car and yourself out into the unending torrent of the beltway. Jim loved it. They dashed into the stream.

The rush hour was already beginning, although the sky was still light. Pink clouds had begun to streak the fading blue of the air. When they got off the freeway and onto the turnpike, the streetlamps had been switched on. They drove down a country road flanked by frame houses.

"What did that map say?" he asked.

"Left by the church, right at the school playing field."

They were supposed to go through three small towns before they came to the driveway of the house but—backtracking from the map—they got lost somewhere around the second one and approached the place from behind. At any rate, that was what they thought.

They sat in the car with the light on and pored over the map. Outside it didn't seem to be much darker, because a fog had begun to mist over the landscape. He blamed her for misdirecting him, while she repeated that it wasn't her fault: not if he'd worked it out so carefully beforehand; she couldn't see all those itsy-bitsy names in the dark, and anyway she'd said for him to go exactly the way he'd instructed her.

"Well," he said, "this should do it. Can you remember left—right—left?"

"Sure," she answered. And so could he; that was just the kind of thing he'd told her back at the house.

He started the car again and turned out the light. They both said, "Oh," and "Look," at the same time. While they'd been going over the map, the fog had thickened to a soupy, gray-blue atmosphere that filled the sky and almost obscured the trees at the side of the road. Jim drove slowly. When the road branched, he said, "Which way?"

"Left—right—left."

They passed three other cars, all coming from the opposite direction. As the third one went by them, he said, "At least it doesn't lead to nowhere."

"Unless it's to somewhere else."

"Meaning what?"

"I don't know," she said. "It just came to me."

"Wonderful. You should be working for the government. Which way now?"

"To the right."

"And there's a street sign up ahead. At last."

When they got near enough to the sign to make out what it said, they saw that it didn't have any writing on it at all. It was white, with a red triangle painted on it, and inside the triangle was a large, black shape.

"That's great," she said. "What's it supposed to mean— black hole ahead?"

"Look, there's another one. The whole damn road's full of them. What's the black thing? Come on, you can see that."

Lisa opened her window. The signs were as closely spaced as trees or ornamental bushes planted along a street to enhance its beauty and give shade during the summer.

She leaned her head out and looked at the black object inside the red triangle.

"It's like a kind of frog," she said, pulled her head back in and shut the window. She'd just realized that she hadn't brought her glasses with her; not that it really mattered for a single dinner party, but she always liked to have them with her in case she had to change her eye makeup under a bad light, or something like that.

"I remember now," he told her. "Its OK. I've just never seen it before. It's one of those special signs for the country."

"What?"

"They signpost all the roads they've got to cross to get to their breeding grounds or spawning places, or something. People run over so many of them when it's the season. They're dying out."

"Frogs?"

"No, not frogs. Toads."

"I hope it isn't their breeding season now. That's all we need."

"Which way at the crossroads?"

"Left."

In fifteen minutes they came to a white-painted wooden arrow set low in the ground. It said "Harper" and led them onto a narrow track. The headlights threw up shadowy patterns of tree branches. Leaves brushed and slapped against the sides of the car.

"This better be it," he said.

"Otherwise we break open the wine and get plastered."

They lurched along the last curve of the drive and out into a wide, graveled space, beyond which stood a building that looked like a medievalized Victorian castle. Lisa giggled. She said, "So this is where your friends live."

Jim reached into the backseat for the wine and said he hoped so, because otherwise it was going to be a long ride to anywhere else.

❧

THE DOOR WAS opened by someone they couldn't see. Jim stepped forward into darkness and tripped. Lisa rushed after him. There was a long creak and the heavy door groaned, then slammed behind them.

"Are you all right?" she asked. She fell on top of him.

"Look out," he said. "The wine." It took a while for them to untangle themselves. They rose to their feet like survivors of a shipwreck who suddenly find themselves in the shallows.

They could see. They could see that the hallway they stood in was weakly lit by a few candles, burning high up on two separate stands that resembled iron hat racks; each one expanded into a trident formation at the top. The candles were spitted on the points.

Lisa turned to Jim, and saw that a man was standing in back of him. She gave a squeak of surprise, nearly blundering against a second man, who was stationed behind her. Both men were tall, dressed in some kind of formal evening wear that included tails; the rest of the outfit looked as if it might have been found in an ancient theatrical wardrobe trunk. "Your coat, sir," the one next to Jim said. He held out his arms.

By the time their coats had been removed and the bottle plucked from Jim's hands, they were ready for anything.

One of the men led them down a corridor. Like the hallway, it was dark. The floor sounded as if it might be tile. The air was cold and smelled unpleasant. Lisa reached for Jim's hand.

The tall man in the lead threw open a double door. Light came rushing out in a flow of brilliance. In front of them lay a bright, inviting room: glass-topped tables, gilded mirrors, chrome and leather armchairs in black and white, semicircular couches. There were eight other people in the room. They'd been laughing when the door had opened on them. Now they were turned toward Jim and Lisa as if the room had become a stage set and they were the cast of a play.

"Your guests, madam," the first butler said. He snapped the doors shut behind him.

A woman who had been standing by the mantelpiece came forward. She had on a long, blackish velvet gown and what at first appeared to be a headdress, but which—seen closer—was actually her own dark hair piled up high; lines of pearls were strung out and perched in wavy configurations along the ridges and peaks of the structure.

Jim let go of Lisa's hand. She could feel how embarrassed he was. He'd be fighting the urge to jam his hands into his pockets.

"Um," he began, "Elaine—

"We thought you'd never get here," the woman said. "I'm Isabelle."

She took his hand lightly in hers and let it go again almost immediately. Then she repeated the action as Jim made the introductions. Lisa realized that although the woman was certainly middle-aged and not particularly slim, she was beautiful. But something was wrong with the impression she gave. She had enough natural magnificence to carry her opera diva getup without appearing ridiculous; and yet she seemed out of date. And the touch of her hand had been odd.

Isabelle introduced them around the room. Dora and Steve, the couple nearest to them, were gray-haired. Steve wore a gray flannel suit that might once have been office regulation but at the moment looked fairly shapeless. Dora sported a baggy tweed jacket and skirt. Both husband and wife were pudgily plump, and they wore glasses: his, an old-fashioned pair of horn-rims; hers, an extraordinary batwing design in neon blue, with rhinestones scintillating at the tips. It came out in subsequent conversation that the two were schoolteachers and that they were interested in the occult.

Isabelle gave no hint as to the marital status of the next four people introduced: who was paired with whom, and in what way. There were two women and two men. The women were both young: Carrol, a plain girl with long, straight orange hair and a knobbly, pale face; Jeanette, pretty and brunette, who had shiny brown eyes and a good figure. She was an airline stewardess.

"And Dr. Benjamin," Isabelle said.

The doctor bowed and said, "Oh, how do you do." He was a small, stooped man, just beginning to go white at the temples. He reminded Lisa a little of the father of a girl she'd been to school with.

"And Neill. You probably recognize him." The young man Isabelle indicated gave Jim and Lisa each an effortless, charming smile, just specially for them. He said, "A lot of people don't watch TV."

"I'm afraid we don't," Jim said. "We get home tired, and then we eat." And then they jumped into bed, or else they did that before eating, or sometimes before and after too, but they hadn't watched much television for months.

"Are you in plays and things?" Lisa asked.

"I'm in a megasoap called *Beyond Love.* The cast calls it *Beyond Hope,* or sometimes *Beyond Belief.* It really is."

"What's it about?"

"The short version, or the twenty-three-episode breakdown?"

"We all adore it," Isabelle said. "We miss it dreadfully now that the electricity's going haywire again. We were hoping to watch it over the weekend."

"Just as well you can't," Neill said.

"Not another shooting? They aren't writing you out of the script, are they?"

"I think this is the one where I lose an arm. My illegitimate father whips me from the house, not knowing that—you did say the short version, didn't you?"

Isabelle said she didn't believe any of it and he'd better behave. "And finally," she told Lisa and Jim, as she swayed ahead of them over the satiny rug, "my husband, Broderick." She left her hand open, her arm leading them to look at the man: swarthy, barrel-chested, bald and smiling. He looked like a man of power, an executive of some kind, who relaxed while others did the work he'd set up for them. He was leaning against the mantelpiece. The introductions had brought Jim and Lisa full circle in the room.

"A quick drink," Isabelle suggested, pouncing gracefully upon two full glasses next to a silver tray. She handed them over, saying, "Our very own mixture, guaranteed harmless, but it does have some alcohol in it. If you'd rather have fruit juice—"

Lisa was already sipping at her drink. The glass was like an oversized martini glass but the cocktail wasn't strong, or didn't seem to be. It tasted rather delicate; herb-like, yet pleasant. "This is fine," she said.

"Sure," Jim added. She knew he wouldn't like it but would be agreeing in order to be polite.

"Now, we're going to move to the dining room soon, so if any of you ladies need a sweater or a shawl, there's a pile over there. Or bring your own from your rooms." She said to Jim, "It's such a nuisance—we have to keep most of the rooms a little underheated. Something to do with the boiler."

"Not the boiler," Broderick said.

"Well, pipes, or whatever it is. Poor Broderick—he's suffered miseries over it."

"On the contrary. I just kicked out those two jokers who were trying to fleece us for their so-called work, and that's why we're up the creek now. Can't get anybody else for another three weeks. Maybe it'll get better tomorrow. It ought to be a lot warmer at this time of year."

"It wasn't bad in town," Jim said. "I guess you must be in a kind of hollow. We hit a lot of fog. That's why we were late."

"Yes, it's notorious around here," Isabelle said. "The locals call it Foggy Valley."

One of the mournful butlers opened the double doors again and announced that dinner was served. Jim and Lisa tilted their glasses back. On the way out with the others, Lisa lifted a shawl from a chair near the doorway. All the other women had picked up something before her.

❦

CARROL SAT ON Jim's right, Jeanette at the left. He preferred Jeanette, who was cheerful, healthy-looking and pretty, but somehow he was drawn into talk with Carrol.

The room was intensely, clammily, cold. He started to drink a lot of wine in order to warm himself up. Lisa, across from him, was drinking too—much more than usual.

Carrol kept passing one of her pale, bony hands over her face, as if trying to push away cobwebs. She said that she'd felt very restless and nervous ever since giving up smoking. "I tried walking," she said. "They tell you to do that, but then I'd get back into the house and I'd want to start eating or smoking. So, I knit. But you can't take it everywhere. It sort of breaks up the conversation. And I'm

not very good at it, even after all this time. I have to con-
centrate on the counting." She blinked several times, as if
about to cry.

From his other side Jeanette said, "I guess we're all
looking for different things. Except—I bet really they're
not so different in the long run. In my case it was the
planes. I'd get on and begin the routine, get everything
working right, count the meals, look at the chart, see the
passengers going in, and suddenly I'd just know: this one
is going to crash."

"What did you do?" Jim asked.

"I got off. They were very nice about it when I explained.
They didn't fire me. But they said I had to take therapy."

"And?"

"And I did. It was fine. It was a six-week course and
it really made me feel a lot better. So, I went back to work
again and everything was OK for another year. I thought I
had it licked. And then it started up again, just like before.
That's where I am now."

"What are you doing for it this time?"

"I'm here," Jeanette said.

Jim took another sip of the thick, brownish-red wine. It
tasted dusty and bitter, although it seemed to be fairly potent

too. The bouquet reminded him of some plant or flower he couldn't place. He took another swallow. His feet were beginning to feel cold. "You mean, here to relax?" he said.

"I'm here to consult Isabelle and Broderick."

"Oh. And is that helping?"

"Of course. They're wonderful."

"They've helped me too," Carrol said. "No end."

The two cadaverous butlers managed the refilling of the wineglasses and the serving of the meal, the main course of which was a stew that they ladled out of an enormous green casserole.

Lisa looked longingly at the food as it started to be passed around. She wished that she'd taken two shawls with her instead of one. It wasn't just the cold, either, or the general darkness of the room; there was a distinctly disagreeable, dank smell emanating from the corners, from the floor under the lovely old rug. Perhaps there was some reason, connected with the low temperature, for the odor: mold, or that kind of thing. She'd suspected at first that it might be coming from the wine, which she'd nearly choked on; it was like taking a mouthful of plasma. Neill had asked for, and been given, two more cocktails. She was thinking that she should have done that herself, when he handed both glasses straight to her without asking if she wanted them.

She'd been seated between him and Dr. Benjamin. She turned her attention to the doctor first. "Are you a medical doctor?" she asked.

He said no and told her what he was, which she didn't understand. "Algae," he explained. "Pond life, biology." Then he made an encompassing gesture with his right hand and arm, adding, "But it's all connected, you know. The animal kingdom, the vegetable kingdom, fish, flowers, rocks, trees. Fascinating. We're only part of it."

"Oh," she said with delight, "yes." She'd caught his enthusiasm and all of a sudden she was drunk. She said to Neill, "I think I got a better deal on the cocktails. It's just hit me. What's in them?"

"I should have warned you—they're pretty strong. The ingredients are a closely guarded secret, but the rumor is that they're dill, parsley and vodka, with a squeeze of lemon and a touch of aniseed. But mostly vodka."

"Nice. Better than the wine."

"The wine is an acquired taste. You'll get to love it."

One of the butlers put a heaped plate of the stew in front of her. A rich, spicy aroma steamed up into her face.

She looked toward Isabelle, who had lifted her fork, and dug in.

The food was nearly as strange as the wine. The meat had a tang like game. "What is it?" she asked, after she'd chewed the first mouthful.

"Chicken livers, I think," the doctor said. "Delicious."

Lisa continued to eat. Surely they didn't make chickens that big. And anyway, the pieces of meat were so chewy and tough, you could almost imagine that they were parts of a bat.

"I've never tasted any chicken livers like this," she said.

"Oh, it's all health food," Dr. Benjamin assured her. "The flavors are much stronger and more natural. Our jaded palates aren't used to them."

"Except the wine," Neill said. "It isn't one of those health wines."

"Quite superb," the doctor agreed, raising his glass. The two men smiled at each other across Lisa. She bit down on another piece of her meat and hit a horny substance that resisted. It was too slippery to get back onto her fork again. She chewed rapidly, then gave up, reached in, quickly took it out of her mouth and put it on the side of her plate. It was a large, rubbery black triangle of cartilage. Her glance darted to the side. The doctor had noticed.

"Wonderful stuff," he pronounced. "Terrific for the spleen."

"If you can get it that far," she said.

"It's good for the teeth and gums to have to chew."

"That's true," Neill said. "I've got caps. Anything happens to them, it's my salary in danger. But I've never hit a bone in this house. You can relax." He began to talk about the degree to which a television actor was dependent on his face, how you began to look at yourself completely dispassionately, as if seeing a mask from the outside. And then you stuck the emotions on afterward. To do it the other way—beginning with the emotion and building toward the outward expression—was so exhausting that you could kill yourself like that, or go crazy. "You can go crazy in any case. I started to flip about three years ago. That's why I'm here."

"I thought actors were supposed to like pretending and showing off."

"It was the series. Autosuggestion. I got to the point where I'd think the things they were making up in the story were actually happening to me. Those characters in the soaps—they really go through it, you know. It was like living that crap. It broke up my life. Broke up my marriage."

"You got divorced?" she asked. "Separated?"

"It started with a coldness. Then there was an estrangement."

He stopped speaking. The mention of cold had made her conscious once more of the chilling damp. It seemed to be pulling the room down into ever darker and deeper layers of rawness.

"Then," he said, "she took the children and left, and got the divorce."

"That's awful," Lisa said. She looked at him with sympathy, but he smiled back, saying, "It turned out to be all for the best. It's how I found this place. I'd never have known how far gone I was. I wouldn't have tried to get help. Maybe an analyst, maybe not. But now I'm fine."

"How?"

"Broderick and Isabelle."

"Are they doctors?"

"He's a healer. She's a medium. They don't advertise it or anything. They aren't in it for the money, like the fakes."

Just for the power, Lisa thought. She was surprised that a couple who looked as capable as Broderick and Isabelle should be mixed up in the occult. That, she thought, was for people like Dora and Steve.

"I take it you're not a believer," he said.

"Oh, I believe in faith healing. That's half of medicine. Well, not half. Forty-five percent."

"You'll come to see the rest, too," Dr. Benjamin told her complacently. She felt angry suddenly. She didn't know what she was doing at this stupid dinner, with these weird people, in a freezing room and eating such revolting food. Even the liquor was peculiar. She tried to catch Jim's eye, but he was stuck with Carrol.

The dessert arrived: a minty sherbet that hadn't set right. The constituents were already separating, and the areas not beginning to melt were oozing and slimy. Lisa took one bite and left the rest. The aftertaste was peppery. Jim finally looked at her from across the table. He gave her a defeated smile. She almost made a face back.

"Coffee in the living room?" Isabelle asked the table. She stood up. Everyone followed. Lisa went straight to Jim. She whispered that she hoped they'd be cutting the evening short, right after the coffee. He nodded and whispered back, "You bet."

"They're some kind of psychic health freaks," she said.

"They cure people of psychosomatic things. Fears and stuff."

"I've got a fear of horrible food."

"Jesus, yes. Even the rolls and butter."

"I didn't see them."

"It was sort of like trying to eat my jacket."

They wanted to stay together but Broderick moved them to chairs where they'd be near the people they hadn't sat with at dinner. Lisa was expected to talk to Dora; the heat of the room felt so good that she didn't mind. She attempted to look interested, while Dora spoke about the difficulty of finding a really good nursery. For several minutes Lisa thought they were talking about children.

She was handed a cup of coffee and lifted it to her lips. It was black, scalding, acrid, and didn't taste like coffee. It was like trying to drink a cup of boiling urine. She set it back on its saucer and looked across the room. Isabelle's neat hands were still busied with the silver pot and the cups. Carrol was actually drinking the stuff; so were Neill and Jeanette and Dr. Benjamin. Dora's husband, Steve, was positively slurping his with enjoyment.

She watched Jim take his first swallow. His nostrils flared, his eyes screwed tight for a moment.

"And that's the most important thing, isn't it?" Dora said.

"What?"

"The soil."

"Of course. Basic," Lisa said. She knew nothing about gardening. When her sister had been out in the backyard helping their mother to do the weeding, she'd stayed indoors to draw and cut up pieces of colored paper. She said, "Do you teach botany at your school?"

"Biology."

"Like the doctor."

"He's a specialist. Most of his work is done through the microscope."

"I guess a lot of his job must be finding out how to get rid of all the chemical pollution around."

"It's a crime," Dora said. "Is that your field?"

"I work for a museum," Lisa told her. "I help to plan the exhibition catalogs and everything."

"How interesting."

It wasn't actually very interesting so far, because she was right at the bottom, just picking up after the other people who did the real work. But someday it was going to be fine: she'd travel, and do her own designs, and be in charge. The only trouble would be trying to fit everything in so that it worked out with Jim.

She could see that Dora was about to go back to biology when Jim stood up at the far end of the room. Lisa said, "Excuse me just a minute." She got up and joined him.

He was talking to Isabelle, who had made him sit down again, beside her on the couch; she was saying, "But you can't." She looked up at Lisa. "You can't possibly just run off. You're staying for the weekend."

Lisa sat next to Jim. She said, "Just for dinner, I thought?" She took him by the arm and dug her fingers in.

"It's very nice of you," he said, "but we must have gotten the signals wrong. We don't even have a toothbrush between us."

"Oh, we can lend you everything."

"And Aunt Alice tomorrow," Lisa said, "and Mrs. Havelock at church on Sunday." She'd used the same made-up names for the past year; ever since the evening when she'd flung a string of them at Jim and he'd repeated them, getting every one wrong. Now they had a private pantheon, Aunt Alice, Mrs. Havelock, Cousin George, the builders, the plumber, the twins, Grandmother and Uncle Bob, Norma and Freddie, and the Atkinsons.

"I'm afraid it's too late in any case," Isabelle said. "The fog here gets very bad at night around this time of the year. I don't think you'd be able to see your hand in front of your face."

"It's true," Jeanette said. "I took a look before we sat down. It's really socked in out there."

"If it's anything urgent," Isabelle suggested, "why don't you phone, and stay over, and then you can leave in the morning. All right? We'd rather have you stay on, though. And we were counting on the numbers for tomorrow night."

Jim turned to look at Lisa. If the fog was worse than when they'd arrived, there was probably nothing they could do. He said, "I guess—"

"If we start off early in the morning," Lisa said. "It's nice of you to ask us."

"I'll show you the way right now," Isabelle told them.

෴

LISA STARED AT the huge bed. It was the biggest one she'd ever seen and it was covered in a spread that looked like a tapestry. The room too was large; it seemed about the size of a double basketball court. Everything in it was gloomy. All the colors were dark and muddy. The main lighting came from above: a tiny triple-bulbed lamp pronged into the ceiling above the bed and worked from a switch by the door. There was also a little lamp on a table at the far side of the room.

"This old place," Isabelle said. "I'm afraid the bathrooms are down the hall. Do bear with us. We try to make up in hospitality. Broderick simply loves it here—his family's been in the district just forever. But I must say, I can never wait for the holidays. Then we go abroad to Italy. When the children come back from school."

"How many children do you have?" Lisa asked.

"Three boys. I don't know why I keep calling them children. They're already taller than their father—hulking great brutes."

Isabelle led them down the corridor to a bathroom that was nearly as big as the bedroom. There was a giant tub on claw feet, a toilet with a chain, and a shower partly hidden by a stained plastic curtain. The place was tiled halfway up to the high ceiling. In the corner opposite the toilet the tiles were breaking apart or disintegrating as if the cement had begun to crumble away.

Isabelle said, "I'll just go see about getting you some towels. We'll meet downstairs. All right?" She left them standing side by side in front of the bathtub.

Lisa whispered, "Some friends you've got."

"It's pretty weird."

"It's unbelievable. What was that stuff we were eating?"

"Jesus, I don't know. I kept trying to guess. I got something on my fork I thought was an ear, and then a hard piece that looked like part of a kneecap. It all tasted like . . . I don't know what."

"They're crazy, aren't they?"

"I doubt it. Pretentious, maybe. Dora and Steve are the crazy types: dull and normal on the surface, but really looking for leaders to show them their occult destiny."

"She's got a thing about soil. God, I wish we didn't have to stay over."

"At least it's warm up here," he said. "And they're right—it's like pea soup outside."

"First thing in the morning, we leave. Right?"

"Definitely. I get the strangest feeling when I'm talking to Broderick, you know. And Isabelle, too."

"I know what you mean."

"I mean really. As if there's something wrong. As if they're the wrong people, or there's been a mistake."

"I've just thought of something. Wouldn't it be funny if you didn't know them at all?"

"Well, I don't. They're friends of Elaine's parents. Or of her mother's cousin. Something like that."

"I mean, maybe we took the wrong road. Are you sure they're the right people? That sign we passed: the one that had a name on it—that isn't their name, is it? Or the name of Elaine's friends, either."

"Well . . . I don't know what we could do about it now, anyway."

"It really would be funny, wouldn't it?"

"And embarrassing. It would be just about the most embarrassing thing I can imagine."

"Oh, not that bad. Not after that fabulous meal they just gave us. And the coffee; how do you suppose they cooked that up?"

"Maybe they had those two butlers out in the pantry just spitting into a trough for a couple of days."

Lisa pulled the shower curtain to one side. "Look at this," she said, holding it wide to inspect the stains, which were brown and might almost have been taken for blood-stains. "The whole house." She pulled it farther. As she drew it away, she could see the corner of the shower. A mass of dead brown leaves lay heaped on the tiles. "See that?" she asked.

"Smells bad too," Jim said.

They both stared down. Lisa leaned forward. Suddenly the leaves began to move, the clump started to split into segments.

Her voice was driven, growling, deep into her throat. She clapped her hands to her head and danced backward over the floor, hitting the opposite wall. Then she was out of the door and down the hallway. Jim dashed after her. He'd just caught up with her when they bumped into Isabelle.

Isabelle said, "Good heavens. What's happened?"

"Toads," Lisa groaned. "A whole gang of them. Hundreds."

"Oh dear, not again."

"Again?"

"At this time of year. But there's nothing to worry about. They're harmless."

"They carry viruses," Lisa babbled. "Subcutaneous viruses that cause warts and cancers."

"Old wives' tales," Isabelle laughed. "You just sit down and relax, and I'll deal with it." She continued along the corridor and down the stairs.

Jim put his arm around Lisa. She was shivering. She said, "I can't stay here. Jesus. Right in the house.

Thousands of them. Please, Jim, let's just get into the car and go. If we're fogged in, we can stop and go to sleep in the backseat."

"We can't now," he said.

"Please. I'm grossing out."

"Just one night," he told her. "I'll be with you. It isn't as if they're in the bed."

"Oh, God. Don't." She started to cry. He hugged and kissed her. He felt bad for not having been able to resist the temptation to frighten her. It was so much fun to get the reaction.

"Come on," he said. "I'll try to find you a drink."

"Oh boy," she sniffed. "Some more of that wonderful coffee."

"They've got to have a real bottle of something, somewhere. If everything else fails, I'll ask for the one we brought with us."

He led her back to the brightly lit living room. Broderick stepped forward with a glass in his hand. "Say you forgive us, please," he begged. "And take just one sip of this."

Lisa accepted the glass. She raised it to her lips. She wanted to get out of the house and go home, and never remember the place again. She let a very small amount of the liquid slide into her mouth. It was delicious. She took a big gulp.

"Nice?" Broderick said.

"Terrific."

"Great. We'll get you another." He pulled her over to the couch where Neill was sitting. Neill began to talk about making a TV film in Italy one summer a few years ago: Broderick and Isabelle had been there at the time. And Broderick talked about a statisticians' conference he'd been attending.

Everyone began to drink a great deal. Lisa felt wonderful. She heard Jim and Carrol and Jeanette laughing together across the room and saw Dora and Steve sitting on either side of Isabelle, the doctor standing behind them. She had another one of the drinks, which Broderick told her were coffee liqueur plus several other things. She laughed with pleasure as she drank. She wanted to hear more about Italy and the museums and churches she'd only ever seen pictured in books. It would be so nice, she said, to go there and see the real thing in the real country.

But why didn't she? Broderick thought she certainly should: go to Italy as soon as possible; come with them that summer and stay at the villa. "Oh, wouldn't that be nice," she told him; "wouldn't it be just like a dream? But Jim's job. And mine too. . . ."

There was a break. She came back, as if out of a cloud, to find herself in a different, smaller room, and lying on a couch with Neill. She knew she was pretty drunk and she had no idea if they'd made love or not. She didn't think so. They both still had all their clothes on. Her head was heavy and hurting.

As she moved, he kissed her. She sat up. He reached toward her. She could see under his shirt a red patch composed of flaking sores. It looked as though the skin had been eaten away. "What's wrong with your chest?" she said.

"Makeup allergy. Badge of the trade. Come on back."

"I think I'd better be going. I'm pretty plastered."

"So's everybody."

"But I'd better go." She got up. He let her find her way out alone. She stumbled through hallways in near darkness, thinking that any minute she'd fall over or be sick. She came to the staircase and pulled herself up, leaning on the rail.

The bedroom was empty and autumnally moist. There was a smell, all around, of rotting leaves. A pair of pajamas and a nightgown had been draped over the foot of the bed. The sheet was turned down. She got undressed and climbed in.

The light was still on. She was thinking about having to get up again to turn it out, when Jim lumbered in. He threw himself on top of the bed, saying, "Christ, what a night. Where did you get to? I looked everywhere."

"I don't know," she said. "I feel terrible." She closed her eyes. When she opened them again, he was already sleeping. The light was still on. She turned her head and fell asleep herself.

When she woke again, the room was in darkness and stiflingly hot. The odor in the air had changed to one of burning. "Jim?" she said. She started to throw the covers back. He wasn't anywhere near. She felt around in the dark. It was so pitch-black that it was like being trapped in a hole under the ground. What she needed was a flashlight; they'd brought one with them—the black one—but it was still in the car. "Jim?" she said again. She sat up and clasped her knees. She was about to peel off the borrowed nightgown she was wearing, when he touched her hands.

"I can't sleep," she said. "It's so hot."

His hands moved from her finger down to her shins, to the hem of the nightdress and underneath it, up the inside of her legs, and rested on her thighs. She held his arms above the elbows. He sighed.

She said, "Let me get out of this thing," and was reaching down and back for the nightgown hem when a second pair of hands slid gently up the nape of her neck, and a third pair came forward and down over her breasts. Close to her right ear a fourth person laughed. She yelped. Her arms jerked up convulsively.

They were all on top of her at once. She whirled and writhed in the sheets and yelled as hard as she could for Jim, but they had their hands everywhere on her and suddenly she was lifted, thrown down again, and one of them—or maybe more than one—sat on her head. She couldn't do anything then; the first one had never let go of her legs.

She couldn't breathe. Two of them began to laugh again. She heard the nightdress being ripped up, and then, from a distance, the doorknob turning. Shapes bounded away from her across the bed. Light was in her eyes from the hall. And Jim was standing in the doorway. He switched on the ceiling lights.

She fell out of the bed, onto the rug, where she knelt, shuddering and holding her sides. She whined about the men: how many of them there were and what they'd been trying to do to her. The words weren't coming out right.

"What's wrong?" Jim demanded. He put down a glass he'd been carrying.

"Where were you?" she croaked.

"I went to get some water. What's wrong?"

"Men in here—four, six maybe, a whole crowd of them."

"When?"

"Just before you came in."

"They left before that?"

"The light scared them."

"Are you OK?"

"I guess so," she said.

He made her drink half the glass he'd brought back. "Which way did they go?" he asked.

"They're still here. Unless they ran past you when you opened the door."

"No," he said. He looked around. "There isn't anyone," he told her. "Look. Nobody here. Just us."

"They're under the bed."

"Come on."

"Take a look," she ordered. Her teeth started to chatter. She wrapped herself in the torn pieces of the nightgown.

He got down on his knees and peered sideways under the bed. "Nothing," he said.

She joined him and took a long look herself.

"See? Nobody," he said. "Nothing. Not very clean, but no other people."

"They were here."

"Look at your nightgown," he told her. "How much did you have to drink, anyway?"

"Not enough for all that."

"We could both use some sleep."

"I'm not staying in this room unless the light's on. I mean it. If you want the light out, I'm sleeping in the hall: I'm running out of the house. I won't stay here."

"Take it easy. You want the light on, we'll keep it on."

"And the door locked."

"I thought they were still in here."

"The door," she shouted.

He went to the door, which had a keyhole but no key. He pretended to be twisting something near the right place, and returned to the bed. He got in under the covers and put his arms around her.

"I can't wait to get home," she said. "Tomorrow. As early as possible."

"Um. But we might stay just a little."

"No."

"Broderick was telling me about this business deal he's got lined up. It sounds really good. We could travel, everything."

"Jim, we don't even know them. And this whole house is completely crazy. And all this occult crap, and—Jesus, nearly getting raped the minute you walk down the hall."

"I think we all had a lot to drink."

"Not that much."

"I didn't mean you. If there was anybody, maybe they thought this was the wrong room. Maybe it's part of that occult stuff they were talking about at dinner."

"Oh?"

"That would explain it, wouldn't it?"

"If you call that an explanation."

"There are even people who spend every weekend that way."

"Sure."

"They do."

"Not in this part of the world."

❧❧❧❧❧

BRODERICK SAT AT the head of the breakfast table. He'd finished eating, but drank coffee as he read the papers. He was still in his pajamas and dressing gown. At the other end of the table Isabelle poured tea. She wore a floor-length housecoat that had a stand-up collar. Her hair was pulled high in a coiled knot.

They were in a different room from the one in which the last night's dinner had been laid. The windows looked directly onto a garden, although nothing was discernible of it other than the shadow of a branch next to the panes. Everything else was white with fog.

"Tea or coffee," Isabelle said, "or anything you like. Just tell Baldwin or Ronald if you don't see what you want on the sideboard."

The other young members of the party weren't yet down. Dr. Benjamin was seated on Isabelle's left. He dipped pieces of bread into an eggcup. Dora and Steve sat side by side; he was eating off her plate, she was buttering a piece of toast. "I just love marmalade," she said.

"Is it always like this?" Lisa asked, looking toward the windows.

"It's a little worse than usual today," Broderick said, "but it should break up by lunchtime. We'll just have to keep you occupied till then. Do you swim? We've got a marvelous swimming pool. Really. Art Nouveau tiles all over. This place used to belong to—who was it? A real dinosaur. But the pool is great. And it's got three different temperatures."

"I don't have a bathing suit," Lisa said.

"We've got lots of extra suits."

Lisa and Jim each ate an enormous breakfast. She looked at him swiftly as they rushed to the sideboard for third helpings.

They almost started to laugh. The food was entirely normal, and the coffee too.

The morning passed pleasantly. Broderick showed them over most of the house. Some of the rooms were light and modern, others old-looking and apparently moldering. "We used to rent parts of it out," he told them. "For a long time that whole side over there was used as a retreat by a religious organization that Isabelle's Aunt Theda was involved with. If we sold it, I guess somebody'd turn the place into a school. They all want me to sell. But I couldn't bear it. My parents bought this house when I was seven. I remember moving in."

There were a billiards room, a game room with Ping-Pong tables in it, a library. The pool was indeed magnificent. Jim and Lisa put on the suits they were offered. Broderick and Jeanette joined them. Neill sat in a canvas chair where it was dry; he said the chlorine made his skin allergy itch. And Carrol, who had sat down next to him, pulled out her knitting and shook her head. She was waiting, she said, for her consultation with Broderick.

Broderick swam for about ten minutes, got out of the pool and went up to Carrol. "Right," he said. She packed up the knitting without a word and left with him. Neill challenged the rest of them to a Ping-Pang match.

It was surprising, Lisa thought, how much she was enjoying herself. But after the Ping-Pong they passed through a hallway that had a window, and she rushed forward to look out. The world was still white, but it was as bright as electric light. The sun was going to burn off the fog quickly.

"We can start soon," she said to Jim.

"Well, not right away. We could stay for lunch."

"As soon as possible."

"It wouldn't be very polite."

"What happened last night wasn't very polite, either."

"Let's not start on that again."

"OK. Let's just get out fast."

"This thing Broderick talked about—it sounds really good. It could make a big difference to us."

"Jim, for God's sake," she said.

"Just cool it, Lisa. There's no hurry." He pushed forward ahead of her and turned to the right. She leaned back against a green stone statue that held a bowl meant for flowers. She wondered if she had the strength of will to get into the car herself and just drive away on her own.

He had the keys. It was his car. And he was the invited guest, even if this wasn't the right house. All the embarrassment would be his to deal with after she'd gone. She couldn't really do that to him.

Jeanette met her at a turn in the corridor. "Are you staying for the season?" she asked.

"I don't think so. We'll be leaving pretty soon. We've got to get back to town."

"That's too bad. The sessions really help."

"In what way?"

"Well . . . just talking. Broderick says that fear—fear itself is a disease. Do you believe that?"

"To a certain extent. Sure."

"It helps to talk about it."

"It helps if the thing you're afraid of goes away. If you can make that happen by talking, I guess that's good."

"Of course you can. Because it's in the mind."

"The things I'm afraid of," Lisa said, "are definitely not in my mind. They're in the world."

"But if they haven't happened yet—"

"A little anticipation keeps us all alive. Right?"

"It keeps us frightened."

"Frightened people are careful. And careful people live longer."

"Sometimes it isn't worth it," Jeanette said.

They reached the breakfast room. Steve and Dora were still at the table. Sunlight streamed in through the windows.

❧❧❧

SHE RAN UPSTAIRS, got her purse and raced down again. She felt wonderful: the sun was out and at last they could leave.

Broderick met her at the foot of the stairs. "Where to, and so fast?" he said. He smiled jovially but his eyes gloated at her.

"We've really got to get back now," she said.

"But Jim said you were staying through lunch."

"I'm afraid not."

"It's all fixed. He said he'd phone whoever it was you had to meet."

"It isn't that simple. Where is he?"

"Out in the garden somewhere, I think. Want me to help you look?"

"No, thanks," she said. "It's all right."

She stepped out the side door onto a brick terrace. Stairs led down to a garden of white-flowering bushes. Beyond them stood a statue of a woman, one signaling arm raised out of her marble drapery. Neill was sitting on a bench at her side.

Lisa asked, "Have you seen Jim?"

"No."

"Who's this?"

"One of those goddesses. Artemis, maybe. Bow and arrow—is that right? I didn't pay much attention in school. Most of the time I was bored stiff. Couldn't wait to get out and see the world."

"I loved it," she said.

"Sit down."

"I just came out to find Jim. We're leaving."

"I thought you were staying till Monday. I hoped you were. Don't go."

"We really have to," she told him, walking away.

He got up and fell into step beside her. He said, "Tonight and tomorrow are the best times. People come from all around. It's when we hold the séances."

"Oh, God," she said. In the distance Jim was walking toward them. He raised a hand. "There he is. I'll just have a couple of words with him." She hurried ahead.

∽ఴఴఴఴ∼

"WE'RE STAYING," HE said.

"Jim, I can't stand another minute in this place."

"Every time I turn around, you look like you're having a great time with that Farley Granger clone."

"Last night I was nearly raped by four men while you were getting a drink of water."

"Last night you were completely pie-eyed and suffering from massive wish fulfillment."

"Oh Jesus, how can you be so stupid? How—"

"We're leaving right after dinner, but if it's too late,

then we'll go in the morning. Whatever happens, we're definitely staying till the late evening, because Henry Kissinger's invited."

"Who?"

"Ex-Secretary of State, Kissinger, a name you may have seen in the papers?"

"What are you talking about?"

"He's coming here for dinner tonight."

"Why?"

"Christ. Because he was asked, of course."

"Well. Well, so what?"

"Look, Lisa: I see nothing wrong about name-dropping, and if I get a chance to sit at the same table with a name like Kissinger, a part of American history, I'm sure as hell not going to miss it. Are you? Isabelle says he tells wonderful stories. Come on, Lisa, are you with me or what?"

"Give me the keys," she said.

"Keys?"

"I'll drive back, and you can get a ride with Henry Kissinger or somebody else."

"Of course not. It would be unforgivably rude."

"I don't believe he's coming."

"He is."

"I'll make a scene."

"Hah."

"I'll say I recognize him from photographs as the Nazi commandant of a concentration camp. I'll—"

"Lisa," he said, "you just shut up and be nice. It's been a little strange, but you're going to have to take it. I've got an important deal on with Broderick and if you mess things up, believe me you're going to be sorry, because I won't stand for it."

He'd never spoken to her like that. She felt her whole body, and especially her face, go rigid with fury and desperation. She wheeled around and ran off across the lawn.

She reached the front drive and slowed down. It wasn't yet noon, the sun was bright; she could walk through all the country roads until afternoon, and by that time she'd hit the highway and find help. She'd phone the police or the Automobile Association, or a friend from town, to come get her.

She settled into a regular stride. It wasn't going to be easy in her party shoes, though they weren't too high and so far felt comfortable. Her lips moved but she wasn't actually muttering. She was thinking about all the times he'd been in the wrong and unfair to her—how this was really the limit and it would serve him right.

She plowed through a muddy field of deep grass and came out onto the driveway. It took her a lot longer than she'd expected to reach the road. Everything looked different in the daytime. In fact, it all looked beautiful. If the house hadn't been such a perfect replica of Haunted House Gothic, the setting could equally well have accommodated a fairy-tale palace. Everywhere she looked there was a superabundance of blossoming hedges, gnarled trees, mossy banks and starry flowers. She began to feel stronger as she went on, despite the shoes: a long walk over stony and uneven ground wasn't going to do them any good— she could tell that already. They'd be ruined afterward for anything but rainy days.

She hummed a little. She reached the road and stopped, looking from left to right and rubbing her hands. She realized suddenly that she'd been scratching at her hands for a long while, trying to get rid of an itch in the folds between her fingers. She'd made all the itchy places bright pink. Red spots like the beginnings of a rash had come up between two of the fingers on her left hand. Nerves, she thought; or possibly a reaction to the peculiar food from the night before.

She turned to the left. For five minutes she walked without seeing a car or a person. Then ahead, coming toward her from around the next corner, she saw two men: rough-looking, bearded and wearing dungarees. She felt apprehensive straightaway. She wanted to turn around and go back. Should she look at them, or past them; say hello, or what? What could she do to make them walk on and not take any notice of her?

One was short, the other tall. They didn't look right at her as they went by, but they were fooling. Almost as soon as she'd passed they were back again, one on each side of her, walking in her direction and near enough, if they wanted to, to grab her arms.

"Looking for something, girlie?" the short one said.

"No thanks, I'm fine," she answered in a small, tight, terrified voice that made her even more frightened.

"Well, we'll just walk along with you a ways," the big one said. "Keep you from getting lonely. Just in case something was to happen to a nice little girl like you."

She looked up quickly. They were both grinning. Would they just terrorize her, or did they mean to act? Maybe they'd kill her afterward, so she couldn't identify them. Maybe they meant to kill her anyway, just for fun. She'd never be able to run fast enough. It was probably better to give in as soon as possible and die quickly.

If she were strong, at least she'd be able to hurt them back somehow.

The little one was beginning to jostle her. They were ready to start; pretty soon his friend would be doing it too. She stepped back and to the side, saying, "Well, if nobody's going to leave me alone today, I might as well go back to my friends. They were right behind me " She began to walk back, in the direction of the house.

They turned and came with her.

"Now isn't that a shame?" the tall one said. "She doesn't like our company."

"That really hurts my feelings," the short one told him. She was itchy and sore all over now. It was difficult to keep walking.

"You think she meant to be mean like that?" the small one asked. "You think she's one of those stuck-up bitches that takes it out on you?"

"I think maybe that's just what she is," the big one said. "I met plenty like her. I know her type."

Her pulse was drumming in her throat and the hairs rising on her arms. Surely it wouldn't happen. It couldn't happen, because she was having such a hard time simply continuing to breathe that long before they started to drag her across the road, she'd have a heart attack. She hoped she'd have one—that everything would just stop all of a sudden and be no more.

She took her eyes from the surface of the road and looked toward the turning. In front of her, emerging from a thicket of bushes to the left, were two people who waved. "There they are," she called out, and sprinted ahead. She could run after all. But she stopped when she was a few yards away. It hadn't occurred to her that she might really know the couple. Now she recognized them: it was Dora and Steve.

"Friends of yours?" Steve said.

"I never saw them before." She turned and looked back. The two men were gone.

"I didn't think they looked very trustworthy," Dora said. "This is a lonely road. You'd better come on back with us."

"So, you're a friend of nature too?" Steve asked. He had a notebook and ballpoint pen in his hand, field glasses hanging from a strap around his neck. "This is wonderful country for it. Best in the world. That's the other reason we keep coming here."

"I can't stay," Lisa told him. "We were only coming for supper last night, that's all. I've got to get back. For private reasons. And now Jim won't even let me go by myself. But that's silly. It isn't fair. I was trying to walk it."

"In those shoes?" Dora said. "Oh dear."

"You have a car here, don't you? Could you drive me? Just to a bus stop or a train station?" She scratched violently at her hands.

"You've got that chlorine reaction too," Dora said. "I've got an ointment I can lend you."

"I just want to get home," Lisa wailed.

"But you wouldn't want to miss the party. You know who's going to be here tonight, don't you?"

"This is important. It's a family matter. Couldn't you?"

"All right," Steve said. "Of course. Right after lunch. Just let us finish the notes first, otherwise we'll have to start all over again. That's soon enough, isn't it—say, just before three? I'd make it earlier, but this is a working weekend as well as pleasure. We're compiling a book—did I tell you?"

"Oh?"

"Toads."

"Dear little things," Dora said. "And fascinating."

"You could stay indoors and do all the research you need," Lisa said. "They're in the house too "

"What do you mean?"

"In the upstairs bathroom, in the shower. There was a whole nest, a big pile of them. Last night."

"Don't tell me they got out?" Steve said.

"It must be another batch," Dora told him. "Ours were fine this morning. I guess you're lucky they didn't nip your toes when you were stepping in there. They're carnivorous, you know." She laughed in hearty barks that ended in a whoop of amusement.

Lisa said, "Thanks for telling me."

They came in sight of the house. Dora said she'd go get that tube of medicine, and added that she couldn't believe Lisa was really going to run off and miss the opportunity of meeting Henry Kissinger. They walked around the terrace to the far side, passing as they went a line of large, brand-new and expensive cars parked against the balustrade. Steve said the cars belonged to patients.

"You'd be surprised," he told Lisa, "how many people consult Broderick and Isabelle. In all walks of life too: movie stars, politicians, big businessmen—you name it."

"Kissinger?"

"I think he's just an ordinary guest."

"Norman Mailer was here last weekend," Dora said. "He talked for hours about glands."

"Hormones," her husband corrected.

"And Henry Fonda before that."

"He's dead," Lisa said.

"Well, maybe it was the other one."

"Which other one? The son?"

"Gary Cooper. Or was it John Wayne?"

"I think we're getting all these names a little mixed up," Steve explained. He winked at Lisa.

"Anyway," Dora said, "he was very nice."

⤳⤳⤳

THEY HAD A cold lunch of food that once again, like the breakfast, was good: salads with chicken, ham and beef; fruit and ice cream afterward. The coffee looked all right too, but Lisa didn't want to try it.

Jim wouldn't look at her. She heard a long account from Dr. Benjamin about tree frogs in Africa. He examined her hands and told her there was nothing to worry about: all the redness was simply a result of friction. As she listened, she could see Carrol, only four seats away, scratching and rubbing herself, touching her face all the time.

She said to the doctor, "Steve and Dora are giving me

a ride back to town at three, but I'm in kind of a hurry. I'd like to get away sooner than that. Did you come by car?"

"I came with them," he told her. "And I think Broderick picked the two girls up on his way out from town. Why don't you ask him? I'm sure he'd run you in."

"I'd hate to bother him," she said. "We'll see."

She went upstairs to wait till three. She paced all around the bed, looking carefully at the dark edging of the heavy, brocaded spread. She sat down on top of it, inspected the material and then slowly prepared to curl up. She lowered her head, but she kept her shoes on. She slept for a few minutes, waking up in a rush as soon as she heard someone walking down the hall.

Jim opened the door, shut it behind him and came over to her. He said, "What's wrong with you?"

"I want to go home. Please, Jim. Remember the food last night?"

"It was fine just now."

"And the cold, and the smell. Those animals in the shower. And I mean it about what happened when you left. You don't believe me, but you don't believe anything from me anymore."

"I'm not staying here for an accusation session."

"Just let me have the car keys, for God's sake. What difference is it going to make to you?"

"If you walk out of here, if you're rude, if you make a scene—it makes me look bad."

"No, it doesn't. I act on my own."

"You're here with me."

"I tried to leave. I was going to walk. Look at my shoes. Two guys on the road tried to grab me."

"Uh-huh. Guys trying to grab you every time you turn around."

"Just let me get out, Jim. Please."

"We're leaving Monday morning."

"Monday? This is only Saturday."

"We've been invited for the weekend."

"Well, if this is even the right house, it was only supposed to be supper on Friday. I don't have a change of underpants or anything. Neither do you."

"Isabelle says she can let you have whatever you like."

"What I'd like is to get back to town."

They argued back and forth in a normal tone at first, then in whispers, and nearly shouting. He wanted to know how she could be so parochial as to leave just when Henry Kissinger was about to arrive: wasn't she interested in world politics, in history?

She said, "You don't believe he's really coming here, do you? To eat mud soup and old tires? Him and Norman Mailer and John Wayne and all the rest of them? They just want to get us to stay here, that's all."

"Why?"

"I don't know. They just do."

"You mean, they're telling us lies?"

"Of course they are."

"But why would they do that?"

"Because they want us to stay."

"It doesn't make sense."

"Does any of it? Look at me." She held out her hands. The skin was patched with pink lumps. "Look at my hands," she told him.

"What have you done to them?"

"I haven't done anything. They're itching because of something in this house."

"Oh, Lisa. I don't know what's gotten into you. Try to calm down."

She stood up. "Right," she said. "Steve and Dora can

give me a ride. And now I know how much I'd be able to count on you." She snatched up her purse and looked at her wristwatch. It said four-thirty. "God, I'm late. Oh, God."

"That settles it."

"Yes. I'll see if they'll still do it. And if they won't, you'll have to."

"Nope."

"And if you don't, we're through."

"That's up to you. You're going to feel pretty foolish when you look back and see how unreasonable you're being."

"And I'm calling the police."

He stood up and threw her back onto the bed. "Everything you want," he hissed at her. "Always for you and never for the both of us, never for me. Who's going to have to build up a career and pay off the mortgage and all the rest of it, hm? You won't cook for my friends, you won't do this or that—"

"And what about you?" she screeched. "Leave me there with a list of all the errands I've got to run for you; I've got a job too, you know. You're a grown man. You can wash your own goddamn socks once in a while."

"You aren't going to give me that women's lib stuff, are you?"

"Just this once—just get me out of here and I'll do anything. You can come straight back, if you like. Please."

"Don't cry like that. Somebody could hear you."

"Please."

"All right," he said.

She sprang toward the door. He followed slowly. They went down the stairs together, Lisa running ahead.

Isabelle was standing at the foot of the staircase. She was dressed in another long, dark robe and her hair was even more elaborately arranged than on the night before. This time the string of pearls that twined through the pile of stacked braids included a single jewel; it hung from the center parting onto her forehead. It looked like a ruby, surrounded by tiny pearls. "And where are you two off to?" she asked.

Lisa said, "I'm sorry, Isabelle—I really am. It's been so lovely here, but we left town thinking it was just for supper last night. I had three people I was supposed to see today, and now I've got to go—I've really got to. The others are going to be furious. I'll have to patch that up somehow, but my mother"—her voice quivered. "My mother's operation comes first. I've just got to get back. We should have said straightaway. Jim—" she turned to him; he could do some worrying for a change, after putting her through all this: "Jim thought you'd be upset if we refused your hospitality. I was sure you'd understand. He can stay, of course. But my mother can't wait, I'm afraid. Not even for Mr. Kissinger."

"That's another disappointment. He just called. He can't make it tonight. Maybe tomorrow, he said. Such a shame. We look forward to his visits so much."

"Tomorrow?" Jim repeated. He sounded hopeful.

"Not for me," Lisa insisted.

Broderick had appeared at the end of the corridor, the other guests grouped behind him. He began to lead them all down the carpet toward the staircase and the light. "What's this?" he said.

"Lisa wants to leave us," Isabelle told him.

"I don't want to. I've got to, that's all. My mother's having a serious operation."

"When?" Broderick asked.

"On Friday afternoon they told me it was going to be tonight, possibly tomorrow morning. I've got to get back."

"I can drive you," Broderick offered.

"Thanks, but Jim's going to."

"I know the roads around here. And I'm used to the fog. Have you seen what it's like?"

"We waited for you," Steve complained. Dora, beside him, asked, "Where were you? You said three."

"I couldn't find you," Lisa said. She suddenly didn't believe that they had waited, or that Henry Kissinger had ever been on the guest list, or that she was going to be allowed out of the house, which was definitely the wrong house. She put her hand on Jim's arm. Her fingers, her whole arm, trembled.

"Why don't you phone the hospital?" Isabelle suggested. She picked up the receiver from the telephone on the table next to her.

They were going to try to fake her out, Lisa thought. But she could phone a taxi, or even the police, if she wanted to. Or—a better idea—a friend: Broderick was undoubtedly on good terms with all the lawyers, doctors and policemen in the neighborhood, as well as any local politicians who lived nearby. "That's a good idea," she said. She let go of Jim's arm and came down the last few stairs.

Isabelle put her ear to the receiver. She said, "Well, wouldn't you know it? It does this sometimes in a thick fog. It's gone completely dead."

Me, too, Lisa thought. She turned to Jim and said, "I mean it. Now."

He spread his hands toward Isabelle. "I'm really sorry," he said.

"Another time," she told him. She shook his hand and smiled. She shook Lisa's hand too, holding the friendly look and the smile.

Broderick called after them, "Come on back if the fog catches up with you. They can be dangerous. People can actually choke to death in them."

∽✆✆∾

ALL THE AIR outdoors was smoky. They got into the car. Lisa said nothing, although she felt safe already. If they had to, she wouldn't mind sleeping in the backseat. At least they'd be away from the house. Jim turned the key. He drove the car across the gravel. Lisa waved at the dimly lighted doorway.

They moved down the drive, along the woodland road and out onto the highway, where almost immediately they hit the real fog. Jim went very slowly. The fog came toward them in long strips like white veiling that kept tearing in pieces or bunching up around them.

"What was all that about your mother?" he said.

"I had to think of something they couldn't explain away. It would have looked bad if they hadn't been sympathetic."

"Isabelle was very nice about it."

"She was mad as hell."

"She was not. She was kind and understanding."

"And she has Kissinger for dinner just all the time—oh, yes. And what a surprise: the phone doesn't work."

"What are you getting at?"

"Those weirdo people holding occult meetings together."

"They're wonderful people. They're studying phenomena that can't be explained yet by any of the scientific principles we know of so far. How do you think anyone ever gets to know things, anyway? There's always a time when it sounds crazy and crackpot—when it's all being tried out experimentally. As soon as a thing's accepted, then it's considered normal."

"You think that house is normal?"

"Well, the heating's kind of erratic and the pipes don't work so well, and what do you expect? It's a big old place down in the country. It'd cost a fortune to fix it up."

"It wouldn't cost a fortune to give us tuna salad to eat, instead of whatever that horrible stuff was. It wouldn't—"

"Wait," he said. All the windows had suddenly gone stark white. The effect was blinding until he turned off the lights. He slowed the car to a crawl. "If it gets any worse, you'll have to walk in front, to show me where the edge of the road is."

"No. We can just stop here and sleep in the car. Pull off the road."

"You heard what Broderick said about the fog."

"I don't believe it."

"Well, I do."

"I'm not going back there, Jim," she said.

"Jesus Christ," he shouted, "what's wrong with you?" He stopped the car and switched off the ignition. "I think you're crazy," he said. "I really do. Just like your whole damn family."

"OK. You can think what you like, as long as we never have to go back to that place."

"This is the end of us, you know. I can't go on with you after this."

"If we just get home, we'll be all right."

"You screwed up everything with them. I don't know how anybody could have behaved the way you did. Completely hysterical, and lying your head off. It was obvious."

"But does that mean I've got to die for it?"

"Die? Nobody's going to die."

"And why do we have to split up? Why do they mean more to you than I do? You didn't even know them before yesterday."

"I guess maybe I didn't know you very well, either."

"Oh, shove that."

"Uh-huh. Nice."

"You know me. And you know how I feel about you."

"Maybe not." He opened his window a crack. They could see the white fog creep in like smoke. He tried the lights again. This time the glare wasn't thrown back, but the lights didn't seem to penetrate more than a few feet into the shifting areas of blankness.

She said, "When you got up for that drink of water last night, where did you go?"

"Down the hall to the bathroom."

"You were with somebody else, weren't you?"

"No," he said. "But it's a good idea."

The whiteness became all-enveloping. The temperature began to drop inside the car. The sound of rain seemed to be coming from somewhere, though they couldn't see any.

"I don't understand," she said, "how you could have let us get into all that."

"It was too foggy to drive back. It was like this."

"And this morning, when I asked you for the keys?"

"This morning you were already crazy; people grabbing you left and right. If this doesn't clear soon—"

"We sit it out."

"I suppose so." He was about to cut the lights, when something dark thudded against the windshield and was gone again.

"A bat," Lisa called out.

"No. It didn't look . . . I think it was rounder. Maybe a bird. I guess the light attracted it."

There was another sound as two more of the things struck Lisa's side window. She undid her seat belt and moved near to Jim.

He was watching the glass in front of him. Several more of the dark shapes hit. They sounded like rubber balls being thrown against the car, all over the metal parts suddenly: on the roof too. He leaned forward. "Frogs," he said. They were everywhere, bouncing up and down, lying still, or slithering across the glass.

"Not frogs," Lisa moaned. "Toads."

"Jesus, will you look at them—there must be hundreds."

"Thousands," she said. "Oh, my God."

He turned off the lights. It didn't have any effect. The toads continued to bombard the car.

"Maybe if we start moving again," he said.

"We can't. They're jamming themselves into the exhaust. Can't you hear them?"

"I could really step on it and blow the muffler off." He switched the engine on again, turned the lights high.

Now the toads were all over. They blocked the view from the windows. They were also a great deal bigger than before. When one of them landed, it sounded like a soccer ball.

He started to drive. The exhaust pipe roared, the car inched forward. He tried to use the windshield wipers, but the toads hung on until the blades stuck in one position. There were swarms of the animals, uncountable. Clusters of them lay squashed or flattened on the windows. And the big ones crashed down on top of them. A dark liquid began to run over the panes.

"Could they break the glass?" she asked.

"I don't know. It's safety glass. They might be able to bang into it hard enough, if they all jumped together."

"They're carnivorous," she said.

ON ICE

ON
ICE

BEVERLEY MOVED TO Munich during the late summer. She found a room with a German family, enrolled as an auditor at the university and got to know her way around the town. In the evenings she went out with her German boyfriend, Claus.

They had met the year before, on the boat coming over; they'd all—her parents too—been traveling on a charter deal that had worked out cheaper than most air fares at the time. Claus had been going out with an older girl in the big crowd she'd been with, but he'd given her his address. And so when the family was back in America, she'd looked him up.

In the spring he'd asked her to marry him. She'd said yes. From the moment of meeting him she hadn't considered anything else: that he could leave her, or that one of them might die, or that he might have been the kind of man to seduce girls and leave them flat or to carry on two affairs at the same time. She hadn't really considered much at all. She'd simply thought she'd stop living if she couldn't be with him.

He was ten years older, already a settled man: a doctor. Because of his work she didn't see as much of him as she'd have liked to; sometimes he couldn't tell when he'd be on duty. He'd show up late. In fact, he was hardly ever on time for anything. She accepted the fact that it was the job that was to blame. Since she loved him, she didn't question it. Once he turned up two days later than he'd said he would.

Now they were together nearly all the time. They had separate addresses and they ate their meals out, but she was pretty sure that in another two months or so they'd announce their engagement officially and maybe get married in the spring, or at the beginning of the summer. She wanted to go to college, but that too would work out somehow.

He had taken his holiday so that they could spend Christmas and New Year's together. He'd booked the rooms and everything. She bought a parka and a pair of ski pants and was looking forward to the trip. She'd never been on skis.

The night before he was to pick her up, she packed her suitcase, turned out the lights in her room and took a last look across the street at the steep roofs and studio apartments opposite. A thin layer of snow lay in patterns over every ridge and line. The light was off in the glass-roofed atelier where a dark-haired young man—probably a painter or sculptor—lived on his own. She used to see him from time to time when she passed by the window, or stood there to open the inner panes and put her milk and butter next to the outer ones to keep cold. One day he had waved frantically at her. And, instinctively, she had ducked away out of sight. Afterward she'd been furious with herself, and wanted to see him again so she could wave back, as she should have done in the first place. But he was never there. It upset her that she might have hurt his feelings—that she'd been so prim and suspicious. That was the way she was, unluckily, because that was the way her family liked people to be, especially women. That was the way she was with everyone but Claus.

He arrived early, for once. His skis were strapped to the top of the car; she'd have to hire a pair when they got to the village. The weather was good for driving and Claus was in a lighthearted mood. They kissed as the car went up and down the hills, around the corners. They couldn't wait till Christmas to give each other their presents, so they stopped and opened them in the car. They'd each chosen the same thing—a scarf. But he so clearly preferred the one he'd bought for her, even telling her he didn't think much of the other's color scheme, that she said, "Well, they're both the same size. We can switch." She took off the one he'd given her and handed it to him. It was a gesture of anger. She didn't imagine he'd want to take her up on the offer.

"I suppose we might as well," he said. He held up his scarf and smiled at it. Beverley too liked her own choice better, but she would never have said so. She would never have been so brutal to someone she was fond of. On the other hand, she realized that he didn't often dare to be honest with anyone. It was like her reaction to the painter living across from her: not being able to wave back.

They drove right over the top of the big mountain passes and pulled up near a lookout station where three tourist buses were parked. Some of the sightseers were out exploring the gravelly surface of the glacier formations left over from the Ice Age, some were gathered around the hut that sold soft drinks and sandwiches. Claus and Beverley got out and walked to the gray mass of gritty material on the far side of the road. The air seemed to be colder when they reached it, the sun to go in. It wasn't at all the way a glacier out of the past should look. It was curved like the back of a turtle; dull, dirty and—as Beverley said—reminiscent of ordinary concrete. She was disappointed. She liked old things to have an air of splendor and romance.

Claus, in contrast, was mildly interested. Facts appealed to him. He didn't care so much about looks, although he was always telling her that something she'd be wearing wasn't straight, and he'd often put out a hand to neaten her hair. He was shocked that she could get along with a safety pin instead of taking the trouble to sew back a button that had come off. She could go for weeks without mending something torn.

He couldn't understand such habits and behavior. The slovenliness of it all horrified him. But she knew that her carelessness was one of the things about her that most attracted him. Secretly he would have liked to be more bohemian, to live in the artists' quarter, never to have to say yes-sir, no-sir to the top surgeons who came around on inspection in the mornings wearing white gloves, who shook hands with everyone from top to bottom of the building and then, according to popular belief, peeled off the gloves, flinging them away for the assistant to pick up and take to the laundry or, perhaps, destroy. She was sure he had dreams of tearing all his buttons off and going to work covered in safety pins. He hated his own respectability while prizing the public and cultural disciplines that forced people into repression. He was civilized and he was frustrated. Beverley cured the frustration while he was curing other people's illnesses.

On the other side of the pass they followed the route of the mountain stream—a swift, icy green torrent that raced along beside them. "This is more like it," she said.

The village they were in was down in the valley. Up on the peaks were several larger, more fashionable and more expensive winter resorts, including the famous Hotel Miramar, whose rooms were said to be like art galleries for the *art nouveau* period.

Their hotel was small and overcrowded. Their room was actually not in the main building at all but in what was obviously a private house let out to accommodate tourists and make the owners some money during the season. There were many places in the world where a family could live for the rest of the year on what the house brought in during a few weeks of skiing, or sailing, or whatever was the main attraction of the region. A lot of the Cape was like that, back home.

The hotel dining room was in the main building and had space enough for twenty tables, some seating four people. Theirs was just for two. The food was good—a combination of German and Italian cooking, and there was a lot to eat. The crisp, clear air and the exercise made Beverley hungry all day long.

Claus took her out on a slope where they could be alone and taught her how to ski downhill. It was much easier than being on the T-bar lifts, but even so, she spent most of her time picking herself up. He hadn't taught her how to turn a corner. When she began to go so fast that she was about to crash, she'd fall down deliberately, to save herself, and then get up and start over again. She wished that she had short skis like the ones they gave children to practice on. All the children she saw could ski better than she could.

They spent Christmas Eve in the hotel. The proprietor, a wolfish-looking man with suave manners, smiled amiably at them. He leaned over their chairs to talk to them about the weather and the state of the snow. His name was Lucas, but when speaking of him between themselves, they referred to him as Lupus, because of the way he looked.

There were three other couples in the dining room. Christmas was a time for the family. Those who had chosen to leave their relatives went out to the bars and dancefloors in search of crowds to replace them. Beverley started to drink more and more, to think about her parents opening their presents. She also wondered how much Claus loved her and whether she was always going to be able to get along with him, not to mention his family. She'd met his mother once and couldn't stand her. But that didn't matter; she loved him. She'd never love anyone else. Tears came into her eyes.

"What are you thinking?" he asked.

"About our Christmas scarves. It isn't right."

"I thought you didn't like mine."

"You were the one. You didn't like mine. I'm sorry. I thought it was so nice. And I actually do like it better. But I want the one you chose for me. Don't you understand?"

He said yes, he did. And they gave back their scarves on the way out, so that instead of having what they liked and being unhappy about it, they were happy despite not liking what they had.

After Christmas the whole village filled up fast. They'd been lucky to get in quickly and rent the skis. Every pair in the place had now been claimed by someone. There were people standing in line and looking at their watches for skis to become free. The nightlife too speeded up. The frozen alleyways were full of partygoers on their way to and from the taverns. There was singing in the evenings; you could hear voices calling across the snow, laughter from all the doorways as people burst from lighted interiors into the cold night air and the whiteness of the snow that retained its shine even in the dark.

The best hotel down in the village was the Adler. It also had a good restaurant, very large, and a beer cellar. A painted wooden eagle hung over the doorway and everything inside was cheerful and spotless. You could tell it was the kind of place that would have geraniums in windowboxes when the weather turned warmer. They went there twice for dinner. On the second evening, just as they were leaving, a voice called out in English, "Bev—hey, Bev-er-ley!"

She turned around. She didn't know for a moment which face to look at. Someone was waving at her. She stepped forward. And there was Angela, a friend from school, with five other American college kids all her age. It was unexpected; until that moment it had been unthinkable to Beverley that both her lives, one on either side of the Atlantic, should suddenly join up. She felt strongly that although she had always liked her fairly well, Angela should really have stayed in America.

"Hi, Beverley."

"Hi, Ange. What a surprise."

Angela quickly introduced the other friends: Darell, Tom, Mimi, Liza and Rick.

Beverley had to introduce Claus.

"Sit down," Angela said. "Join us for a beer." She looked at Claus invitingly. Beverley spoke to him in German, saying that they had to meet friends: didn't he remember?

"Gee," Angela said, "you sure can rattle it off, can't you?"

"Sort of," she said. If you couldn't speak another language after a year in bed with a foreigner, you might as well give up. "Where are you staying?" she asked.

"Here."

"For how long?"

"Another week."

"I'll be in touch," Beverley said. "Tonight I'm afraid we've got to meet some people." She headed toward the door again. Claus followed. When they were outside, he asked her why she hadn't wanted to stay.

She tried to explain: about the way it was back home, the gossip, everything. To run around on European vacations with your friends and probably—like rich Angela—be fooling around with all of them, was one thing; but to be falsely registered in a hotel as the wife of a foreign man ten years older than you were, was another. Nobody at home would understand. It wasn't the way people behaved there.

"I bet it is," he said. "I bet they do it all the time, like everywhere else."

"But certain things are illegal. In the state I come from it's even illegal to buy a contraceptive if it's for preventing pregnancy. You can only get them on the excuse that they're to prevent venereal disease. It's all to do with religion. It's supposed to be a country with a secular government, but all the laws about sex assume it's something bad. Unless it really is bad; if it's rape, you need two independent witnesses to prove it. I just don't know that I want to spend all our holiday drinking beer with those people, do you?"

"Of course not," he said. "Why are you so upset?"

She put her arm around him and said she wasn't upset. But he was right, she realized. She hated it that the others had discovered her secret, happy life.

⌁⌁⌁

THE NEXT DAY, after lunch, he told her that he wanted to try one of the high slopes and get a good run down the mountainside.

"I asked Lupus about the timing, but it depends on the snow. I may be a little late. You could go see your friends at the Adler, if you like."

"I'll wait at the room for you," she said.

It was nearly dark when he came in. He was laughing. He stripped off his clothes, wrapped himself in a towel and went across the hall to the bathroom, where they had an enormous tub as big as a bed.

He'd fallen several times. She gathered that it had actually been very dangerous, and there wouldn't have been anybody else around if he'd been seriously injured.

"Look," he said, picking his ski pants up off the chair. "They're all ripped. That's my only pair too. I'll have to ski in my suit."

"I'll sew them," she offered. She got out the pocket sewing kit she'd bought because it looked pretty. The only things in it she'd ever used were the safety pins, although everything was there: needles, thread, a few buttons and a thimble. She sat on the chair and sewed up the long tear in the material while he changed his clothes.

"It isn't very straight," she said. The stitches were large, the sewing like that of a child. The mend resembled a badly healed wound. But Claus was delighted. "As long as it holds together," he told her, and she felt proud of herself.

At supper he said he thought that the next day he'd try the neighboring run.

"Are you sure it's okay?" she asked. "If it's so risky, and there isn't anybody else around? You could break a leg."

"Doctors don't break things. It's like lawyers—they never go to law."

"Lawyers can choose. They don't do it, because they know what it costs. Anybody can break a leg."

"Will you mind being alone down here?"

"No, that's all right."

"You could go up the mountain to the other hotels."

"I could even go to the really fancy place, couldn't I? They probably don't let anyone in that isn't a guest."

"They'd let you into everything except the hotel, I think. That's a good idea. I wouldn't mind going up there too. You can tell me what it's like. I just want to get some real exercise first. You never know what the weather might do."

She said all right: she'd go up to the big hotel the next day.

෴

A MAN WHO worked one of the ski lifts pointed out the right road to her. She was glad of her good German, which was perfectly understood even where the populace spoke more Italian and had grown up with a local language that hadn't mixed with other European tongues since shortly after Roman times. She had heard fellow Americans asking directions in English and having a spate of the home-grown dialect loosed off at them.

She bought a chocolate bar to eat later, instead of lunch, with a cup of coffee. She'd become almost addicted to a particular kind of milk chocolate that had pieces of nougat baked into it. The bar was triangle-shaped and each wedge a triangle when broken off.

She had a quiet ride up. The cable car was large, painted a dark green. There were three other people traveling with her—a young boy who carried a pair of skates, and an old couple, very well-dressed. The woman was carefully made-up, her fur coat looked soft and bushy, her fur-trimmed boots were the kind you wore for sitting down on the observation platform rather than trudging through the snow. Her husband's coat had an astrakhan collar that matched the hat he wore. The cane he held between his knees was topped by a silver knob worked to resemble a piece of wood with knots in it. Both man and woman looked as if they belonged up at the top of the mountain, at the luxury hotel: Beverley wondered why they had gone down to the valley at all. They began to speak quickly in a language she couldn't place.

She looked out of the windows at the blazing white plains and fields, the long swoop of drifts that ran from the crests to a point where the line of the mountainside shot out into infinity. The boy started to whistle and kicked the wall near his seat.

When they arrived at the top, there was a delay. They hung where they had stopped, the doors remaining shut.

The old couple stood up to look. Beverley and the boy were already on their feet.

They could see two stretchers being carried by, the bodies each covered with a white sheet and red blanket; then a third, and the person being carried was fighting to throw the covers off. As the stretcher-bearers hurried past, a hand flung away the blanket and Beverley caught a glimpse of a head entirely red, the crown looking as if it had been cut by an axe, and the mouth open but not producing a sound. She shut her eyes and put her head down. She could hear the old couple murmuring to each other in their own language; they sounded strangely casual, as if the vision hadn't caused them much concern. Perhaps they hadn't seen so much; perhaps their eyesight wasn't very good any more.

When the doors finally opened, she'd forgotten about coffee and the hotel and everything. She thought she'd like to sit down and drink a beer and try to wipe away the memory of the man who'd been hurt. It might even have been a woman—you couldn't tell much from a head and face so badly injured. But she had a feeling it had been a man. And she was sure that he wasn't going to live.

She began to plod along the snow-packed lanes to the center of the village. Just as she was thinking of going into one of the taverns ahead, she came in view of the Hotel Miramar above and beyond her, shining like a castle at the top of the hill. She stood admiring it for a few seconds, then turned into a side street.

She almost skidded on a patch of ice around the corner. Opposite her was a restaurant. She went in and sat down. The waiter was an old man with white hair and a white moustache. He didn't think it unusual that she should order just a beer, alone, in the middle of the morning. A group of men in suits were seated around a table at the back; the place was obviously for locals, not for the foreign skiers. When the waiter brought the beer, she said, "As I came up, in the cable car, I saw a man. Has there been an accident? They were carrying people. Blood."

"Ah, the ice wall," he said. "We warn everybody, but they still have to try it, to prove how good they are."

"What is it?"

"It's a wall of ice in the middle of the toboggan run. If you haven't been braking and using your skill to turn at the corners, you go over the bank and into the wall. It's solid ice."

"They were bleeding all over."

"Ice is very hard. Hard as stone. Hard as steel. The speeds you can achieve going downhill—fantastic."

"Does it happen a lot?"

"Quite often, yes. We try to discourage people from going, but you can't."

She began to drink her beer. He told her that there was another attraction, an ice maze, which was also popular but considerably less dangerous, as the walls were only about a meter high and the gradient not too steep; people used special puffy cushions to slide through it. Children loved it. It was one of the Miramar entertainments that was open to the public.

She asked directions to the ice maze and the skating rink. When she was ready to leave, he came outside the door with her and pointed up the hillside.

It was a long way up. She was out of breath by the time she started to climb the steps. And they were slippery too. The handrail was coated with ice. She wondered what everything would look like in the summer, how different it would be. There were lakes in the neighboring valleys; people would probably be lolling around in deck chairs and trying to pick up a suntan. And the famous skating rink, she suddenly remembered, could be turned into a swimming pool. If Claus ever wanted to come back to the place in warmer weather, she'd be able to join him then up on the mountainside—not that she was an expert at hiking or rock-climbing either, but at least she could go for a long walk. Not knowing how to ski meant that their time was going to be divided. She hadn't thought about that before they'd arrived.

She bought a visitor's ticket and stood by the side of the rink until she felt cold. She was too self-conscious to put on a pair of skates herself. It was all right to watch, but to get out and slide around all on your own would be futile. She couldn't see anyone who was without a friend or relative. Claus was out on the slopes alone, but skiing was different. And he was a man; that made a difference too.

She managed to find a perfect place in the after-ski lounge, a small table next to the vast plate-glass window that overlooked the rink. She brought two cups of coffee to it, drank one, started on the first section of her chocolate bar and was about to break off another piece when she heard a voice saying, "Well, here you are again."

It was Angela. She sat down in the second chair. She was wearing a top-to-toe outfit made of some silvery, shiny material that looked as if it might have been designed for an astronaut. She pushed her dark glasses to the top of her head, undid the earphones of her Walkman and said it was great running into each other again.

Civilization, Beverley thought, was what stopped people from telling someone like Angela to shove her earphones up her nose and get lost. "Been skiing?" she asked.

"Till I fell on my duff," Angela said.

"Alone?"

"No, the whole gang's here. What about you? Got your Mr. Gorgeous with you? Who is he?"

"A friend," she said.

"Some friend. He looks—you know. All those cheekbones and everything. Really European."

"He is European."

"I mean, like he looks. He looks European. You know?"

"Sure," Beverley said. "Who-all are you with?"

"Oh, just that bunch you saw the other night."

"Who are they?"

"Well, Liza went to school with me those last two years. Tom and Rick are in my class: economics and government studies. Then, Mimi and Darell—how can I describe them?"

"Lovers?"

"No, silly." She gave Beverley's arm a coy little push. "Mimi and Darell are sort of in the group, except they actually didn't quite make it. First of all they were too late, and then she started to have all these doubts. So they aren't officially registered with the organization."

"What organization?"

"The Fountain of Light."

"The what?"

"It's our Christian fellowship foundation. We bring the culture and hope of the free world to—"

Beverley removed the saucer covering her second cup of coffee.

Angela's expression became fixed and devout. She gabbled about "the word," the need for real estate, "the light" and the building of training centers; "the fountain"; the establishing of weekly lectures in notable beauty spots, the investment of cash in long-term plans for truth, light, love and a whole lot else, including medical research. Very few people outside the movement knew, she said, that vitamin intake was directly related to disorders of the personality. But some day there would be "detoxification clinics" all over the world, where people could go to profit from the word.

"To read?"

"To resolve their vitamin imbalance, Bev. To reach God. We'd like to start up an education program right here."

Beverley stopped listening and drank. For Angela to have turned out to be a run-of-the-mill brainless co-ed was bad enough. For her to be part of a maverick cult bringing fountains of light anywhere was worse, though possibly slightly more interesting. She said, "I don't know how much luck you'll have trying to give away culture and hope around here. I think they're all Catholic going back centuries."

"But we all believe in God," Angela said.

"Uh-huh. Did you see the accident? On the toboggan run?"

"I heard about it. It sounded terrible."

"From après-ski to après-vie in two seconds flat."

"Beverley, don't joke."

"I'm not joking. I saw them. It shook me up so much I had to go get myself a drink."

"You saw them? What was it like?"

"Red. Red and trying to scream."

"I don't want to hear."

You just want to ask about it, Beverley thought. She put down her coffee cup and said, "Have you ever seen the ice maze?"

"Of course. It's fun, if you can get into it. All the kids want to play there. It's considered a children's thing."

"But it must be dangerous, if it's ice."

"They have these big pillows they ride on. About the size of a rubber raft. I haven't heard it's so dangerous. Want to try it?"

"Okay," Beverley said. "Just let me go to the ladies' room."

The ladies' room, only one of several in the building, was as full as an airline lavatory of free gift-wrapped soaps, bottles of cream and eau-de-cologne. Beverley took one of everything.

They put on their outdoor clothes again and stepped out onto the long porch that ran the length of the lodge. Spectators sat in deck chairs all along the railings. On the level above, indoors, there was an enclosed verandah for sunbathers, who lay basking behind glass walls and windows that let through the ultra-violet rays. There had been one year when the visitors had read magazine articles claiming that the ultra-violet was just the part of sunlight that caused skin cancers; and the number of sunbathers dropped dramatically. But the next year everyone had forgotten the scare. They wanted to be tanned again.

Beverley followed Angela. As she walked, she thought about how strange it was to be up where all the swish hotels were and the moneyed people who went to places like that only because they wanted to have rooms with a specific look, or a certain kind of food in the dining room and dry martinis at the bar. She passed one woman, an American, who was shouting, "Hector, Hector," at someone; the woman wore dark glasses and a large mink coat. On her hands she displayed an array of massive gold rings set with stones bigger than eyes. Her fingernails were painted red and in her right hand she held a plastic Coca-Cola cup. Why leave America, Beverley wondered, if that was what you wanted? Why had Angela left? Maybe they were people who just didn't believe the places where you took your vacation were part of the real world, especially if the native inhabitants spoke a different language.

They waited in line for two pillows and launched themselves into the ice maze, which was funnier and more exciting than Beverley had imagined, and less tiring than skiing. She sped forward through the glistening runways on her striped cushion and yelled as loudly as the children around her.

Afterward they joined Angela's friends for sandwiches and coffee and then went out on the skating rink. When Beverley said she had to go, they begged her to stay on for tea and supper and dancing. There was a wonderful pool down inside the hotel too. Beverley said no, she had to get back.

"But tomorrow?" Angela asked. "Come on up tomorrow, or meet us early down at the Adler."

"Maybe," she said. She was sure Claus would want to be with her. She hurried as the light began to go. She was worried that he might have been waiting for a long time. But she was the first one back. When he came in, he was smiling, and in an even better mood than the day before. The slopes had been splendid, he told her: simply magnificent. Tomorrow he'd go even higher.

"Will you be all right with your friends?" he asked.

"I guess so." She tried not to act hurt. They had a good dinner and a lot to drink, and went to bed as soon as they got back to their room.

He was up early and kissed her goodbye while she was still in bed. She set her alarm clock and went back to sleep.

For the next three days their separate daytime routines worked out well. He kept finding bigger and better ski runs up in the mountains, and she could tell him all about the hotel, the ice maze, the skating, the heated pool and the game rooms. She also told him that Angela, although she'd never mentioned it again, had confessed to being a member of some weird religious cult.

"As long as it isn't political," he said.

"Those things never are."

"Of course they are. What do you think?"

"Well, in this part of the world it wouldn't matter; only in the East, where they might start handing out Bibles or something."

"What do they believe in?"

"She didn't say exactly, but the name is loony enough. I once had a terrible conversation with a couple of Seventh Day Adventists. I think that's what they were. It lasted three hours and twenty minutes. All this horrible stuff about being the elect. I couldn't get away. I didn't want to be rude. Jehovah's Witnesses, that's what it was."

"Ridiculous. We used to get them at the door when I was in Cologne. You just tell them you're already something—Catholic, Jewish, Muslim—and say you believe in that."

"But I don't. I didn't want to upset them, but I did finally say it didn't matter to me if I wasn't saved."

"But you believe in God."

"Of course," she said. She had to say it because of the first time he'd asked her, in bed. "Do you believe in God?"

he'd whispered; and she had said yes, since she couldn't say anything else, and since what he was really asking her was: did she love him beyond anything. But later she was furious. It was as if in the throes of intercourse she had been asked, "You do believe the sun goes around the earth, don't you?" What could you say? *Let me think about that one.* It was unfair.

He had been profoundly shocked when she'd told him that in accordance with her father's humanitarian principles, she had never been baptized. Her father had believed that people should wait until they were old enough to understand the words said over them, and could then choose whether or not they wanted to join a church.

Claus had said, "But that's terrible. Every civilized human being—"

That was the point at which she had seen that despite his reputation in the hospitals as a rebel and a firebrand, he would always want to abide by the rules he'd grown up with, and that they included strictures of thought as well as of behavior. When he reached up to push her hair away from her forehead, she'd pull a face and tell him, "That makes such a bad impression," or, "What will the neighbors say?" She'd invented a quavery, shaking voice to quote his favorite scolding phrases back at him. But she'd kiss him afterward.

"All this mystic nonsense that's supposed to be masquerading as a religion," he said. "I don't know how you can associate with them. I wouldn't want to be in the same room with people who are so stupid. Fanatics. Like being in the wards for the insane."

"You thought they looked all right the other night."

"Look, maybe. It's the ideas."

"Do you think the idea of life after death is less peculiar than their plans to distribute sweetness and light?"

He talked for a long while about the ineradicable false romanticism of Americans. He said he thought it had something to do with not having lived through a wartime occupation recently, or even a war that had been fought over their territory.

She agreed with him, though she felt that since they were talking about her country, she should have been the one to criticize it. He didn't like it all that much when she had things to say against Germany; he'd tell her that her opinion was interesting but, as he'd go on to explain, somehow misinformed, if not just plain wrong: she hadn't been looking at something in the right way.

They had once had a terrible quarrel—which had gone on all night—about Germany's part in the Second World War. She had become genuinely hysterical, while he'd remained unconcerned. And after that she thought that although she couldn't live without him, she might not be able to stand being married to him. She wasn't really absolutely sure if she could stand being married to anyone: to end up like other married women who were full of recriminations, unfulfilled, nagging; and who spent their time cleaning and scrubbing and having children—all of which she'd come to eventually, of course, though at the moment the idea of such a future, such a fate, repelled her. Marriage was going to be the price of being allowed to stay with Claus.

"That hotel used to be a sanatorium," he told her.

"I'm not surprised. I feel a lot better since I've been swimming in the pool."

"Not that kind. For tuberculosis. A lot of famous people died there. Then they all moved to Switzerland."

"After they died?"

"The famous people started going to Switzerland instead. And after that, people stopped getting TB so much."

"The rich people stopped," she said. "They're giving a big party up there on New Year's Eve."

"Let's stay down here. I don't want to be with a lot of other people."

She didn't want to, either. She'd had enough of the crowds in the daytime—on the skating rink, in the ice maze, along the observation porches. She had also, temporarily, had enough of Angela's friend, Tom, who had taken her over on her second day at the ski lodge and insisted on sticking with her every minute, as if they had been a high school couple. She hadn't asked him about the religious movement, or about much else. He had kissed her in the hotel corridors between the tearooms and the swimming pool, and she had allowed it and kissed back even while she asked herself what she was doing in that group and why she should be letting him near her. She didn't want to have to explain about Claus. Maybe she wouldn't have to, anyway. She and Tom clung to each other against the hotel wallpaper and embraced. He knew how to kiss, all right, but in other ways seemed oddly incompetent. He was utterly lacking in the purposeful manipulations she was accustomed to from Claus. He seemed to be getting excited about her, but to be unwilling to follow through. She even wondered if he'd ever had a girl.

She also wondered why she should need this additional

proof that she was desired. She knew that already. All the boys in Angela's circle approved of her. And she knew why: it was because she had been another man's woman—that was all there was to it. She was prettier than she used to be, and she was a real woman, because of Claus. But Claus had had other affairs before her. She herself had never had anyone else. It put her at a disadvantage with him.

They stayed in their hotel for New Year's Eve. Only four other couples were in the dining room. At midnight the lights were turned out and she kissed Claus in the dark. A local band was brought in, a crowd gathered, and people began to dance. Herr Lucas danced with an old woman who might have been his mother or perhaps his wife. Beverley and Claus swayed slowly over the polished but uneven floor. She was slightly drunk and sleepy and was happy thinking about how much she loved him, how wonderful he was, even the smell of his skin, which drove her crazy; and how everything had to turn out all right in spite of his horrible mother and all the things he didn't want to talk about because he was lazy and it was easier not to think about them if he didn't have to.

Next day, Angela said suddenly, "Are you in love with this guy?"

Beverley was just biting into a sandwich. She nodded.

"Have you really thought about what it would be like to get married to a foreigner?"

"Um."

"Would he fit in?"

"Oh, we'd live here."

"Here?"

"In Europe. Well, that's where he works."

"But—gee, I couldn't stand that. I mean, it's nice, but it's so different. You know."

"That's why I like it."

"But it isn't democratic."

"Is America?"

"Of course. America is a democracy. Where did you go to school, Beverley?"

"For a couple of years, to the same place you did. And then, I was at one of those liberal progressive numbers where you couldn't get in if you weren't the right kind. They used to take a certain per cent of stereotype misfits and minorities to cover themselves, but it was pretty exclusive. I'm glad of it too. I got a good education. Weren't your other schools like that? Or did you sit next to the children of roadsweepers and ditchdiggers?"

"Oh, school. I didn't mean that. I meant the country, and the government."

"Tell me about the Fountain of Light."

Angela said, "It's a lifelong dedication to an ideal, Beverley. It's a force of good in the world."

"Is it open to everybody?"

Angela began to talk about the "Movement," as she called it. Beverley kept a straight face, but only just. From what she could gather, the Fountain of Light wasn't exactly like the Clan, but they were pretty near it. Their favorite word for people who disagreed with them was "degenerate."

"What does that mean?" Beverley asked.

"Psychologically evil and immoral."

"I thought it had something to do with not living up to your ancestors."

"No, honey—it's people that can't live up to an ideal."

"Why can't they?"

"Because they're too degenerate."

"I see," Beverley said. "That explains it."

She asked Tom on their way to the swimming pool, "Do you think I'm degenerate?"

He said, "How do you mean?"

"Aren't you one of the Fountains of Light?"

"Well, yes."

"So, do you think I'm degenerate?"

He looked very serious and said, "Let's put it like this: I think you've fallen into evil ways."

Beverley burst out laughing. She had to steady herself against the wall.

"It isn't funny," he said. "It's a tragedy."

"What's a tragedy?"

"You and that guy you're with. What do you think you're doing?"

She took a deep breath and thought of telling him precisely.

"You must know it's wrong," he said.

"What's wrong?"

"Well, you aren't married to him, are you?"

"No, and I'm not married to you, either."

"That's different."

"Oh? Why do you hold me tight and keep kissing me— do you love me? Are you planning to marry me?"

"Yes," he said.

She was so shocked that she couldn't answer. He took her by the elbow and drew her down the hallway. He put his arm around her and began to talk about the commitment to love and the commitment to God. She felt battered. She couldn't even argue back.

They reached the doors to the changing-rooms. She said, "Even if I were free—"

"You are free," he told her.

"No. I'm bound to him. And I love him."

"You don't love him. If you'd loved him, you wouldn't have let me kiss you."

"I guess that was just because I'm so degenerate," she said.

"We'll talk about it some more tomorrow."

After their swim, he went to join Mimi and Darell on the ski slopes. She lay down on a mattress in the sunroom and fell asleep for a few minutes. She had decided not to return to the Miramar the next day.

∾ಿರಿೂ

WHEN SHE WOKE up, she heard two women talking. They were sitting right nearby on the next two mattresses and were speaking English. She opened her eyes, but she was facing the other way. She was looking at a lot of extremely old men and women in bathing suits. In the past two days the hotel had filled up with some very ancient tourists. It seemed strange that they should come just for New Year's Eve; probably it was for the healthy air more than the celebrations.

"I've told them: we've really got to improve the security," one of the women said. "Anybody can come up here now. Look at what happened last week."

Something about the voice disturbed Beverley. She had the feeling she'd heard it before, but she couldn't remember where.

She turned her head and found herself looking up into a face she recognized. She said, "Oh. Mrs. Torrence," and sat up.

The woman's head moved sharply. She was in her early eighties and she looked actually younger than Beverley seemed to recall, but it was the same woman: a friend of her grandmother, years ago, back in St. Louis. Beverley remembered her from vacations there.

"Who?" Mrs. Torrence said.

"Beverley. My grandmother was—"

"Oh, of course," Mrs. Torrence said. She smiled. She introduced Beverley to the other woman, a Mrs. Dace, who had hair that was dyed red, although she appeared to be the same age as her companion. She smiled pleasantly at Beverley and asked if she was staying at the hotel.

"No, I'm down in one of the villages. This is out of my price range, I'm afraid."

"Then you're all alone up here today?" Mrs. Torrence said.

"I was with some friends till just a little while ago. We'll be meeting for tea as usual, and then go on back down."

"Oh, do join us for tea. We can show you the parts of the hotel you'd never see." She turned to Mrs. Dace and said, "You remember giving little Alma the tour? This'll be just the same. Such fun to have some young faces around."

Beverley didn't want to be impolite. She accepted the invitation. In fact, she was rather looking forward to seeing some of the private suites; they might be ones that retained the original nineteenth-century decor or, even better, have been remodeled in the more famous *art nouveau* designs. The two women would be treating her to the tea; that made a difference too. And, in addition, she'd be able to avoid Tom.

"We can leave a message with your friends, if you like," Mrs. Torrence said.

Beverley wrote a note to say she'd run into someone from home. Mrs. Dace levered herself off the mattress and took the folded paper away; she promised to find an envelope for it and leave it at the reception desk. Mrs. Torrence began to tell a series of stories about St. Louis in the old days when she and Beverley's grandmother were girls. Beverley was delighted. She'd been very fond of her grandmother.

After they'd changed, they took an elevator up to one of the higher floors. Mrs. Dace asked to be called Minnie and Mrs. Torrence said her name was Martha and she'd be angry now if Beverley used anything but her first name from that moment on. She took a gold key out of her alligator bag and fitted it into a door at the end of the hallway. Beverley would never have known that the door led anywhere—it looked from the front like another ordinary linen closet or a place where the hotel maids would keep brooms and mops and maybe some extra sheets. The key, on the other hand, could have been real gold: it was in the form of a winged nymph naked from the waist up; her legs became the part of the key that went into the lock.

"Here we are," Martha said.

They stood in a hallway parallel to the one they had left. The ceiling was higher, the moldings more elaborate, the carpets more opulent. Ahead of her Beverley saw gilding, parquetry, Venetian mirrors and fresh flowers that blossomed from vases set in scalloped niches along the walls. She looked hard at everything, hoarding details to present to Claus later on, when he was back from the skiing and they'd be lying with their arms around each other; she'd tell him stories as if she were a traveler who had returned from foreign journeys: first she'd been able to bring back part of the world that belonged to Angela, and now it would be the places inhabited by the very rich and—so it appeared—the old.

Martha gave a commanding sign with her right arm, leading onward. They entered an adjacent corridor and came to a bank of windows that looked out on a view of ice-covered crags and fir trees going down into a chasm; arched and fluted snowfields hung in roofed masses above them.

"Wonderful," Beverley said. She thought Claus would love it too.

"You can only see it from this side," Minnie told her. "It's reserved for us."

"Shh." Martha put up a warning finger. "Beverley will think we're bragging."

Minnie lifted her hand to her face. She muttered, "Oh. Of course."

Martha led the way into her rooms and then out again, into Minnie's. Beverley was staggered by the apricot satin bedspreads, the green marble sunken baths, the black and silver chairs. They told her the names of the designers and walked her farther along the hallways to a tearoom that looked like the main salon of an ocean liner. Minnie and Martha waved to a few groups at other tables; the men made motions of bobbing to their feet as they bowed forward. All the people were old. There were about fifty of them in the huge room. Beverley wondered if it was like an old people's outing: if Minnie and Martha were members of some sort of exclusive club for five-star holidays. She also had for a moment a sudden sense of isolation and strangeness. If she could have thought of an excuse, she'd have asked to go back. She was almost ready to make something up, to say, "Oh, I just remembered. . . ."

"We generally come in a bunch," Martha said. "We're all friends here." She smiled and added, "Old friends."

Tea came, with both cakes and sandwiches. Beverley began to eat voraciously. She'd worked up a hunger again from the swimming. The two old women watched as if pleased to see someone with such a hearty young appetite.

They talked about the skating and the ice maze. Martha asked Beverley how long she was staying and she answered that it would be only two more days because her friend had to get back to work. "And you?" she said, to keep the conversation going.

"Oh, we both live here most of the year now," Martha answered. "I guess you could say we've retired to the mountains: Took to the hills."

Minnie tittered and said, "Yes, you could say that."

"Don't you miss St. Louis?" Beverley asked.

"I really try," Martha told her, "to live in the present as much as possible. I like reading the papers and looking at TV."

"Well, you could do that at home. You could—" Beverley stopped. She had been about to say something that had to do with how difficult she found it to think of living in Europe forever, not just for a while. She had been getting ready to talk about Claus and her family. Something had sidetracked her. She stared at her teacup. What was it? The feeling of isolation and uncertainty came over her again. She cleared her throat. And suddenly, she remembered: St. Louis. In St. Louis, ten years before, when she was just a child, she'd been to Martha Torrence's funeral.

She looked up.

"Yes, dear?" Martha said.

This time Beverley was deserted by her natural instinct to hide herself before she was certain what was going to happen. She was too surprised to cover up. "Mrs. Torrence—she said.

"Martha."

"In St. Louis. I went to your funeral."

"Yes." Martha sat smiling at her. Minnie was looking away at a corner of the room.

"Yes?" Beverley repeated. She remembered Claus saying: *A lot of famous people died there.* She breathed in. She felt her comprehension slipping. The time passed. She sat in her chair for what seemed like ten minutes, until she knew how to go on. "Was it something to do with the insurance?" she asked.

"How smart of you, Beverley." Martha grinned. You could see that her teeth were the best money could buy; and her cosseted complexion also, helped by face-lifts, no doubt. Beverley thought: *She probably looks a lot better than I do at the moment.*

"Not exactly a swindle," Martha confided, "but shall we say: a conspiracy. I was very fortunate in my doctor— a man who was five years my senior, and what he didn't know about nursing homes wasn't worth knowing. It's rather a long story. Shall I tell you?"

"Yes, please," Beverley said. Now she was intrigued and thrilled. Claus wouldn't mind her being late, once she'd explained why. *Wait till I tell people,* she thought, *that I had a long talk with a woman who died ten years ago.*

Martha glanced at Minnie, who picked up her cup and saucer and said, "You'll excuse me, won't you? Now that you've started in on the explanation, I'll just go say hello to Herbie." She toddled off to a table up against a palm tree by the wall.

಄಄಄಄಄

MARTHA SAID, "A friend of mine had a terrible thing happen to her once. She was in her late sixties and her children were all in their forties. She had grandchildren and two great-grandchildren. It was a large family. And

Ida, my friend, started to lose her memory and repeat things and get confused all the time. The family thought it was premature senility. You can't blame them; what can you do except take the advice of the experts? And in Ida's case the experts said she was deteriorating fast and should be in a home. And that was that. The children were devastated, but there was no choice. They had her put away and they went through the whole legal business of transferring the house and the property and the money, and dividing it up as if she'd already died. She'd been declared *non compos,* you see. And she was, of course. It was all perfectly straightforward. Except for one thing—the nursing home she was in: they automatically gave their patients antibiotics. So, suddenly, eighteen months after the trouble started, Ida was completely normal again. She'd just had some strange kind of infection. Well, maybe you can imagine: she woke up into this imprisonment, not even knowing where she was—or why—and was told that her own family had committed her and taken away everything, even her great-grandparents' silver spoons. And when the doctors came around and discharged her—it wasn't easy, you know. So much in life is a matter of trust."

"Yes," Beverley said, "it's one of the most important things." She was thinking about Claus again, and their dissatisfaction over the Christmas presents. *We each choose for ourselves,* she thought. *But does either of us trust the other to choose for both? And that's what marriage has to be. There has to be that trust on both sides.*

Martha said, "Ida's family loved her very much. It was all a tragic mistake, or rather, a misdiagnosis. But it got me thinking: sometimes people aren't much loved by their families. I started to sound out a few of my other friends and you'd be surprised, you really would be, at how many were honestly afraid of getting pushed down the stairs or handed the wrong medicine, or just scared to death. When you're old—you've got the experience, but if your eyesight starts to go, and your hearing, and you aren't so quick on your feet any more, then it's frightening to know that people who don't like you—who sometimes actually hate you—are just waiting for you to die off, the quicker the better. And you wonder how far they'd go."

"But the medical profession is very careful about that kind of thing."

"The medical profession can mess something up just as fast as anyone else."

"I'm engaged to a doctor," Beverley said.

"Then you'll know I'm right. They misplace the X-rays, they operate and leave the sponge in, sometimes a clamp too, they get the names switched around and cut open the wrong one, they bring mothers somebody else's baby to feed. Isn't that right?"

"All I meant was, if it's a matter of a person's sanity, so somebody else can get the money, then they're very careful."

"So it seems. There are a lot of cases you don't read about because they never get to the papers. There are a lot of families who can't take it any longer. Ask a doctor in his seventies. They know. Anyway, about a dozen of us decided to do something. We formed a society. And now you've seen it."

"You pretended to die, and got part of your money away first, and then you just came here?"

"That's right. We own this hotel and another one in Switzerland and a big place down in the Caribbean—we've got a whole island there—but the climate doesn't agree with everyone; it can be tough on arthritis sufferers. I really like it best here now. Of course, as far as the climate goes, we should really be based somewhere like Arizona, but that's too close to home for most of us. Too dangerous.

We've got quite a big foreign contingent, but the majority of us are still American. There are a lot of us now too. In ten years we've gotten up to about fifteen hundred. Quite a sizeable little club. And now you're one of us."

"Don't worry," Beverley laughed. "Your secret's safe with me."

"Of course it is. Because you'll be staying here. That's why I've been talking to you."

"Staying? How do you mean?"

"You're going to be staying here now, with us. There's no other solution. It's what I was saying about the importance of trust, Beverley—we simply can't afford it. We've broken the law: just think of the tax situation for a start. And on top of that, we'd have the families after us. Impossible. You'll settle down soon. It can be very entertaining here, you know."

Beverley sat back in her chair. She surveyed the people at the other tables, who, she could now see, were darting interested glances in her direction. But maybe she was imagining it. Maybe it was just because she was the one young person in the room. Or—because they all knew Martha Torrence went off the deep end like this whenever she found somebody new to talk to? Or maybe they were all in on it, and this could be some special refinement on a game they played with strangers and outsiders.

She decided to argue it through and find out how much more was to come. She said, "Time is on my side."

"That's true," Martha admitted. "In twenty years, I and all my friends will be dead—really dead. But the movement is very popular now. There are new recruits every year. And every year they're going to be just a little younger than me. Eventually, they'll be your age."

Beverley tried to laugh, and couldn't. She wanted to get up and leave, but she knew she'd never find her way back through the corridors. And besides, she'd need the gold key. When she thought of the key, she felt sick. The picture came back to her with loathsome clarity: of the old woman's well-manicured hand clutching the winged, golden, naked girl and fitting the feet into the keyhole.

"There's nothing to worry about," Martha said. "We've got help from the outside. Maybe you've met some of them—the Fountain of Light movement?"

"What?"

"Of course, they're under the impression that they're fund-raising for other people. It wouldn't be right to tell them the truth. So many young people nowadays need to feel they're part of something grand and important. I don't think they'd appreciate being told that their efforts were really only keeping a large group of very self-indulgent great-grandparents in the champagne and cigars of their choice. The young are so in love with ideals. They might not see the humor of it."

This time Beverley did laugh. That would really be something to tell Claus; and her parents too. She lifted her cup shakily, drank, and sloshed some of the tea into the saucer.

Martha continued, "You'll be completely taken care of. You'll be our pet. I must say, it will be a delight to have a young face to look at. And our old boys will simply adore you. You'll be idolized."

"I'd rather be loved," Beverley said. "Really loved." Tears began to roll down her cheeks. "I'd rather," she said, coming right out with it, "be in bed with my boyfriend."

"I daresay. But one can overcome that. There are other things in life. You'll just have to apply yourself to them."

Beverley put her hand up to rub it across her face. She stared back at the inquisitive old people. "What other things?" she said bleakly.

"Well, we could start off," Martha told her cheerfully,

"by teaching you how to play bridge. Unless you already know how. You could join the tournaments. We've got some marvelous players here."

"I'm pretty strong. I could escape."

"Yes. Unfortunately that's what the others have always tried. They take someone into their confidence and then—it's distressing, but if it goes that far, we have to do something about all of them."

For the first time Beverley believed the whole story. Her room down in the village, the skiers on the slopes, even the genuine guests on the other side of the hotel seemed as far away as if they existed in a different country. The key had gone into the lock and she was separated from the rest of life. "The three people on the toboggan run?" she said.

"I'm afraid so."

She thought back to the swimming pool: the artificial heat and light, Minnie and Martha talking. "And little Alma?" she asked.

"Yes, her too."

"Who was she?"

"She was the girl before you. You see, if you hadn't said anything about remembering my funeral—well, we'd have let you go. Even if you remembered later and told people about the hotel, no one would take you seriously. But your reaction was so strong."

"I remembered the funeral because I went with my grandmother and I was worried about her. She died fairly soon after that. And I do remember that she cried like anything over you."

"You mustn't be angry at me for that. My son-in-law was getting ready to have me certified for the sake of a few hundred thousand dollars. And my daughters would never have gone against him. Never."

"Have you been happy here?"

"Blissfully happy. The peaceful nobility of the mountains—there's nothing like it. The food is delicious, the wonderful air—and we have the most fabulous doctors, of course; the hot springs and the sunrooms: I'm talking now about our own facilities on this side of the building. We only cross over, we only really come out at all, at New Year's, to see all the young people. That's the only thing we miss."

"I'd miss it even more than you would," Beverley cried. "Couldn't you take my word for it that I wouldn't ever tell anybody?"

"We can't. We just can't. You've got to see that. No, dear, it's much too good a story. You could even sell it for money to the papers. I'm afraid not. You'll have to get used to it. Don't look to the others for help—they're a lot stricter about the rules than I am. You just relax now, and accept. I think you'll find it's going to be in your interest to adopt a pleasant and friendly attitude. Try to breathe in the spirit of serenity that these wonderful mountains induce."

When she didn't come back, Claus would try to find her. He'd telephone the Miramar; he'd go down to the Adler to look up Angela and her friends. After that, he'd go to the police. Perhaps that would be the moment for an eminently respectable and distinguished-looking elderly couple to step forward and say, "We saw her heading down the mountain just as it was getting dark. She didn't seem to know how to ski very well and she took the most difficult route." Then the search parties would spread out over the snow, Claus among the number. But no one would really be surprised if her corpse couldn't be found. People disappeared all the time in the mountains, all year long. The mountains were like the oceans in that respect—every season was deadly.

"We aren't even in the danger zone for avalanches," Martha said. "Anyway, long before the unstable periods, the men get out and fire things off to loosen the snow and send it in the right direction. We're well protected in every way." She bent forward, took Beverley's arm and stood up. "You just come on over here," she ordered, "and sit down."

Beverley rose unsteadily. She felt as dazed as if the tea they'd been drinking had been drugged. Once more tears ran over her face. She allowed herself to be steered to the small table where Minnie was talking with an old man. The man stood and bowed as they approached. Martha pushed her gently into the third chair and sat next to her.

Beverley sniffled and raised the back of her hand to her eyes. The old man held out a handkerchief to her, which— after a hesitation—she took. She thought miserably that it was no wonder the other young ones they'd held pris- oner had been willing to risk escape, if not to take the risk meant year after year, forever: never in her life to see Claus again, or to get back home, to see her family; her body and her life unused and unknown.

"Are you ready?" Martha asked. "Good. Now try to remember: the most important thing to get straight about bridge is the bidding."